The GREENWAY

Jane Adams was born in Leicester, where she still lives, but remembers vividly her childhood trips along the real Greenway, located in the Norfolk village of Happisburgh.

She has a degree in sociology, and has held a variety of jobs including lead vocalist in a folk rock band. She enjoys pen and ink drawing, two martial arts (Aikido and Tae Kwon Do) and her ambition is to travel the length of the Silk Road by motorbike.

She is married with two children. *The Greenway* is her first novel. Her second, *Cast the First Stone*, will be published by Macmillan in September 1996.

The GREENWAY

Jane Adams

PAN BOOKS

First published 1995 by Macmillan

This edition published 1996 by Pan Books
an imprint of Macmillan General Books
25 Eccleston Place, London SW1W 9NF
and Basingstoke

Associated companies throughout the world

ISBN 0 330 34631 8

9 8 7 6 5 4 3 2 1

A CIP catalogue record for this book is available from
the British Library

Phototypeset by Intype London Ltd
Printed and bound in Great Britain

*For my family
and for David
'Just a matter of time'*

Prologue

Even the scent was the same. The dust of late August overlaying the green and the faint tang of sea salt still clinging to her skin.

The feelings too. Knowing that they were late and that Aunty Pat had made them promise to be back on time.

In her dream, Cassie glanced back to see Suzie emptying sand from her shoes.

'Come on, Sue!' Cassie's shout was anxious and insistent. Irritable even in her own ears.

'I'm coming, for God's sake. You worry too much, Cassie. What do you think she's going to do?'

She replaced the shoe, wriggling her foot into it without bothering to undo the laces. Suzie never seemed to worry about things in the way that she did. Cassie gnawed at her lower lip, shifted impatiently from foot to foot.

Suzie came trotting over to her.

'Look,' she said sympathetically, 'if you're really that bothered, we'll cut down between the fields, like we did the other day. Then we'll only be a little bit late. OK?'

Cassie nodded doubtfully.

'Right then,' her cousin said. 'Race you!'

Even in her dream Cassie could feel the exertion of that run. The sun, somehow heavy on her back. The way she seemed to breathe the dust thrown up by their running feet. Then the change from concrete hardness to the faintly crunchy springiness of sun-dried grass as they left the narrow road and turned onto the grass verge which marked the entrance to the Greenway.

Cassie always tried to wake up at this point. Always tried to wrench her body from sleep and her mind back to consciousness.

She never could.

Instead, she was forced to relive the events with the same, no, a greater degree of intensity than she had twenty years before. Greater, because at this point the action slowed. Cassie was aware of every blade of grass flattened by her sandal-clad feet. Every twig and leaf from the high hedges which caught at her hair and seemed, with hindsight, to be a warning, telling them to go back and follow the road round to the village. She heard a snail shell crack beneath her feet, glimpsed the shadow of something, a bird maybe, thrust back into the bushes. Caught the softened thud of Suzie's feet chasing hers up the green-carpeted, green-enclosed pathway.

Then, the sudden shimmer, like a displaced heat haze; the feeling of heaviness cloaked around her shoulders, the ground shifting beneath her feet. Dimly, as she fell, she heard Suzie's distant voice calling her name.

Falling, falling.

Cassie, the child, was engulfed in blackness. An absolute, soundless, thick as treacle blackness. She couldn't hear, couldn't see, couldn't breathe.

Then . . . nothing.

Twenty years on, Cassie woke, fighting her way back to the world she referred to as real. Fingers clutching at the bed covers as though they were her only hold on the present.

Cassie sucked air into lungs that seemed starved of it. Forcing herself to breathe deeply and slowly.

She thought that she had cried out, but Fergus slept on beside her, unaware, peaceful. For a moment only she thought of waking him, reaching out her hand to touch his shoulder. Then, she drew back. Waking Fergus never helped. His sympathy only seemed to jar on her senses. Fergus never suffered from bad dreams. He could not understand the strength of them, the fear of the nightmares which dominated even Cassie's waking hours. No. Fergus couldn't help with this.

Silently and slowly Cassie slipped from her bed, opened the wardrobe and felt blindly into the pocket of her oldest jacket. She withdrew a folded piece of paper wrapped in a plastic bag. Fergus didn't know she still had it. She glanced anxiously at him, but he slept on, peaceful as a child.

Cassie took out the paper. It was yellowed with age and much folded, the creases reinforced with tape where the fibres had begun to part. She unfolded it. Laid it flat upon the dressing table, shifting things aside to make room on the cluttered surface.

A police notice. A request for help.

'HAVE YOU SEEN THIS CHILD?' headed the sheet in bold print. Cassie didn't need to read the rest, she knew it by heart, by her soul. The detail, the date and the time of disappearance. The name of the twelve-year-old child.

Turning the paper so that it caught the faint glimmer of the streetlight slanting through the curtains, Cassie stared at the image and through twenty years of lost time, the eyes of Suzanne Ashmore. Cousin Suzie stared back at her.

Chapter One

'Fergus tells me that you know this place?'

Cassie smiled, nodded.

'Yes, I had relatives here, when I was a kid. I used to come and spend holidays with them.'

'Great place to grow up,' Simon commented enthusiastically. 'The sea, beautiful countryside, hardly any traffic. I've seen more kids out on bikes and on their own these last two days than I've seen in years.'

Anna took his hand, laughing at him. 'Simon the romantic,' she said fondly. 'What about the bad side? Bet you haven't thought about the cold weather, winter storms. No night-life. Having to travel fifteen miles or so to Norwich to do your shopping. How about all that then?'

'Oh, come on, Anna, it can't be that bad. There are local shops and as for bad winters, can't you just see it? Raging seas, spray reaching the cliff tops . . .'

'Half the cliffs being washed away . . .'

'Curling up in front of a real fire . . .'

'Having to clean it out every morning before you can light it . . . Typical townie you are, Simon – arrive in the summer, fall in love with a place and see no further than September. One winter here and you'd be back in the city so fast your little legs'd be a blur.'

Dimly, Cassie heard Simon continue to protest, Anna laughing at him. She wandered away from their amiable bickering, the double act, as Fergus called them, and walked further up the hill to where Fergus was standing.

He reached out, wrapped his arms tightly around her and smiled. 'You OK?'

She nodded. 'I'm fine.' It surprised her to find that she really meant it. This holiday had been Fergus's idea and she had dreaded it. But now that she was here, she felt peaceful, at ease.

She turned to face away from him, pulling his arms around her again, standing very close. 'Look. Down there you can just see my aunt's house. Their old house, you know, when they lived here.'

'I know,' Fergus said. He gently increased the pressure of his arms around her, clasping his hands over hers.

'Down there . . .' She hesitated for barely an instant, felt the reassuring warmth of his hand over hers and carried on. 'Down there is what the locals call the Greenway. You can see the line of it, dead straight from the road to the foot of this hill.'

'Hummock,' Fergus said.

'What?'

'I'm just not sure that you could call this a hill,' he explained. 'More like a blip, or an over-ambitious molehill. It's only because this entire place is so flat that it looks like a hill at all.'

Cassie laughed and Fergus squeezed her more tightly.

'You're beautiful,' he said, 'and I'm very, very proud of you.'

'It's not as bad as I thought it was going to be. Maybe you're right, Fergus. I've got to learn to lay my own ghosts, twenty years is a long time.'

The others had wandered up to join them, hands clasped but still bickering.

'Tan's hill,' Simon was saying, waving an expansive arm. 'Know what that means anyone?'

'Oh, God,' Anna groaned. 'Simon's playing school ma'am again.'

Simon ignored her.

'It's a contraction,' Cassie said unexpectedly. ''Tan's hill – St Anne's hill.'

'Very good.' Simon applauded. 'A prize for the lady in the red shirt.' He paused, grinned at her and went on more seriously, 'Actually there are a lot of Tan's or St Anne's hills. Most of them conical or gently rounded.' He made a descriptive gesture with his hand playfully following the contours of Anna's body, then dodging back to avoid the punch she threw at him. He went on, 'Holy places, most of them. You know, pre-Christian. Thanks to dear old Pope Gregory, the more deep-rooted of the local obsessions, the Church just stuck a new label on. Most of the hills with an Anne or Tan label were Danu's hills. She gave power to the land, fertility to the crops, that sort of thing.' He grinned again. 'And poor old St Anne almost certainly died a virgin. Ironic, don't you think?'

'I thought that was virtually compulsory,' Anna

7

commented. 'To die virginal if you were going to be saintly, I mean.'

'Probably,' he confirmed cheerfully, and made a deliberately clumsy grab for her. 'Just glad you didn't follow your namesake, that's all I can say.' He reached for her again, flopping down onto the springy turf and pulling her with him, sharing kisses, until, practicably, Simon's curiosity got the better of the moment and he strained his head back to look at Cassie. 'Is there water around here? A spring or stream or something?'

'Mmm, yes. There's a spring at the foot of the hill, just as you leave the Greenway. Why?'

'What's the Greenway?' asked Anna.

'It's a kind of pathway between those two big fields. Look, you can just see the line of it from here.' She pointed back down the hill towards the darker line of the high hedges against the ripening fields. 'Why did you ask about water, Simon?'

'Because water was Danu's association. Places where she was worshipped were generally near water.'

'Lots and lots of the stuff over there,' Anna commented, waving a hand to where they could just glimpse the ocean over the rise of the cliff edge.

'Not quite the same.'

For several minutes, they were all silent. As Fergus had said, the hill was hardly impressive, but the flatness of the landscape made it a vantage point from which seven churches could be seen. Due east of them, the lighthouse reared skyward. They had earlier passed close by it, walking along the cliff edge and had seen the remains of its predecessor still clinging grimly to the sandstone. Year by year, the sea took a higher tribute, claiming a little more of the coastline. Cassie had been shocked at how much had gone since her last visit here. At how much closer to the cliff edge the flint church now stood. Somehow, she had thought, you just didn't allow for churches, or lighthouses for that matter, dropping off the edge of cliffs. They seemed too big, too solid to be decimated by such insidious corrosion. She had to remind herself that she had been gone from here a long time. A few inches a year over so many years. It added up.

This whole landscape was full of memories.

'See down there?' She pointed to a church, tree-shrouded and seeming to have no attendant village. 'We went ghost hunting there.'

'Ghost hunting?'

'Yes. This area's full of legends. Ghosts everywhere and just about every type you could imagine.'

Simon pulled up a plantain stalk and nibbled thoughtfully at it. 'And what variety of ghost were you hunting that time?'

Cassie laughed. 'Not sure I remember now. Headless coachman or something, I think.'

'Did you see anything?' Anna demanded.

'No. We got cold and wet, it was raining of course, frightened a few motorists and gave up long before midnight.' She smiled at the memory. 'Aunty Pat was always game for that sort of thing. Always saw the funny side. And Suzie . . .' She hesitated then, Suzie's was a name she rarely allowed herself to say out loud. 'Suzie would do anything if it looked like fun.'

She stared down at the Greenway, her hopeful mood suddenly evaporated. Fergus clasped her hand.

'You still keep in touch with them?' Simon asked.

Cassie's answer sounded falsely cheerful even to herself. 'I still see Aunty Pat and Uncle Mike. Not often, but we keep in touch . . . sort of.'

Suddenly, she didn't want to talk any more. She wanted to leave, go home, or at the very least, back to the cottage they had rented. In the pit of her stomach, she could feel the familiar panic, rising now from her stomach to clasp at her chest and throat.

Slowly, she exhaled. Anna was saying something. Cassie forced herself to concentrate, divert her thoughts, her attention, from the familiar red panic haze that seemed to waver, absurdly, somewhere behind her eyes.

'Sorry?' she said, relieved that she had managed to sound almost normal.

'I asked who Suzie is,' Anna told her.

'You all right, Cassie? You've gone very red,' Simon asked her. 'You've maybe been in the sun for too long.'

She forced herself to smile. The panic was receding now, she took her time before answering.

'Maybe we've all been in the sun too long,' Fergus was saying, covering her silence for her. 'I don't know about anyone else, but I'm hungry.'

'You're always hungry,' Anna told him. 'Why you're not twice as fat as Simon, I don't know.'

'Hey, now, just a minute. Are you implying that this body is anything less than perfect?' Simon protested.

Anna grinned at him, poked playfully at the slight flabbiness of his stomach. 'Would I think that? No. But there is such a thing as too much perfection, and this bit' – she pinched the spare flesh, none too gently, making him yelp in protest – 'this bit,' she went on, 'is definitely too much of a good thing.'

She leapt to her feet then and ran away from him. Simon gave chase, pausing to shout to the others that they would meet by the car.

Relieved, Cassie watched them go.

'Are you all right?' Fergus asked anxiously. He placed his hands on her shoulders, strong fingers massaging the tension from them, probing almost to the point of pain. Perversely, Cassie found herself relishing the minor discomfort. She sat still, allowing his fingers to drive the last of the panic-born tension from her body.

'You're handling things really well,' Fergus told her softly. 'Have I told you how much I love you today?'

She leaned back into his arms. 'Not since breakfast,' she said, 'and that was hours ago.'

They sat quietly. Fergus always smelt good, Cassie thought. He bent his head to kiss her, his beard and hair tickling her neck. She rested contentedly against him, allowing his hands and kisses to comfort her.

'We should go,' he said, 'they'll be waiting for us.'

Reluctantly, she allowed Fergus to pull her to her feet, and lead her back down the hillside.

11

Just before they reached the others, he paused, and turned to her.

'Cassie, Cassie love, you're doing so well. If you're really serious about putting this behind you, well, you've got to be able to talk about it in the same way you can talk about other things. However bad it was, sweetheart, it was one incident. One thing in a whole lifetime of things. You've got to be able to see it that way.'

She stared helplessly at him. He wasn't telling her anything new, anything she didn't know.

She nodded slowly. 'All right, Fergus. I promise, I'll try.'

'Simon and Anna love you, Cassie. I love you. We all want to help.' He held her tightly, stroking her thick brown hair. 'It's all going to be fine, Cassie. Everything's going to be all right. Tonight,' he said, 'tonight I want you to talk about it, what happened here on the Greenway.'

Chapter Two

The evening had turned unexpectedly chill. The wind, which had blown from the land throughout the day, had veered seaward and now brought a salt-tinged coldness with it. Anna drew the thin curtain across the seaward window, shivering as she did so.

Cassie laughed. 'It's not that cold.'

'No? Tell my feet that.'

'Might help if you put something on them.'

Anna looked speculatively at her bare toes, wriggled them against the grey of the kitchen flagstones. Then she grinned, crossed the room to sit beside Simon and dumped her cold feet in his lap.

'Best footwarmer in the business,' she said, then frowned slightly and asked, 'You've not been back here then, not since you were little?'

Cassie shifted uneasily, shook her head. 'No. My aunt and uncle moved away, so there seemed no reason to until now.'

'Why now?' Anna pressed her. 'I mean, sure, it's a great place, no complaints there, but why particularly?'

Cassie looked uncomfortably at the floor, tracing the patterns in the faded rug with the toe of her shoe. 'It seemed about time,' she said slowly. 'Last time I was here, well, things happened that I never wanted to think about. It made it kind of hard to come back.'

She looked away, parting the curtain slightly to stare at the thick cloud rolling in across the coast.

Anna looked anxiously at her, conscious that she had somehow upset her friend. It was not Anna's way to pick too closely at what were clearly sore places in another's mind. She scrabbled around for some neutral subject, grasped, unknowingly the one area Cassie had been trying to avoid.

'Tell us more about the hill we were on today. Tan's hill. There've got to be stories about it.'

Simon nodded. 'Those places usually have some kind of legend attached to them. Sometimes they're known as fairy hills; you know, you go to sleep there and wake up either in some other world, or find you've slept for centuries. That sort of thing.'

Cassie sighed and nodded slowly, bowing to the inevitable.

'There are lots of stories about that one,' she said. 'I don't remember them all now, it was a long time ago.' She hesitated again.

'When you stayed with your aunt?' Anna prompted.

'Yes.' Cassie took a deep breath and told herself not to be so stupid. After all, this was what she had come for, wasn't it?

She began to speak again. This time the words came easily, almost too easily, as though they had been long confined in so small a place they now burst free before she closed the door again.

'Aunty Pat said it was a witches' hill. She said that there were records in the vicarage library of ceremonies held there on May eve and sometime around Christmas. Winter solstice I suppose. That was, I don't know, sixteen something, I think.'

'Doubt it,' Simon commented. 'Earlier maybe, or later, late seventeen hundreds. A century earlier, that was the height of the witch mania, they'd be in too much danger to meet openly somewhere as easy to see as that.'

Cassie shrugged. 'I wouldn't know. Anyway, it seems the local vicar decided that it wasn't on and held Christian ceremonies up there instead. I don't remember the details, only that he said that the bonfires were a pagan thing and shouldn't be allowed, oh, and there were some rumours of what he called sexual licence going on up there.' She laughed. 'I remember that bit because Uncle Mike used to joke about not knowing you needed a licence for it. He said they'd probably manage to put a tax on it as well.'

'A tax on sex!' Simon shuddered, poked Anna in the ribs. 'Be bankrupt in the first month.'

Anna slapped his hand away. 'Off, Simon. Go on, Cassie.'

'Well, I don't remember a lot more. The Greenway was supposed to be some kind of ceremonial pathway. I know it's meant to be very ancient. Aunty Pat reckoned that it must have joined the path from the lighthouse at one time, before the farm was built. If you stand up near the old lighthouse and look towards the hill you can just trace the Greenway. I don't know. They do seem to line up. Would there be a reason for it to lead to the sea, Simon?'

He looked thoughtful. 'Maybe. It's very hard to say without being there, seeing the alignment. Danu came from over the sea, but not the North sea. There could have been local associations though, some kind of blessing for the fishermen.' He shrugged. 'There's really no way of knowing.'

'There was an old woman living in the village when I used to stay here. Everyone said she was, you know, a bit touched. Aunty Pat said she knew everything there was to know about the history and legends hereabouts, or, if she didn't know, she'd make something up for the cost of a couple of brandies.' She laughed again, more at ease now. Fergus was right, she must keep things in perspective. 'She claimed that some ancestor of hers was hanged on Tan's hill. Hanged for witchcraft.' She paused. 'It's funny, before that, I always thought witches were burned, but she said not.'

She looked to Simon for confirmation. He shook his head. 'No, the Church made a nice distinction. You had to be a heretic to be worth burning; common or garden witches were only worth the rope to hang them with.'

'Nice people,' Anna commented. 'And I suppose that was after they'd tortured them into confessing?'

Simon shook his head again, raked his fingers through his short blonde hair. 'Strangely enough, no. Not here. In Europe the inquisition got away with pretty much what it wanted. Here, actual torture wasn't normally permitted for suspected witches. We didn't lose out though, our lot just devised their own version. You could say that British witch hunters originated psychological manipulation.'

'How do you mean?'

'Well, you might find yourself locked up, alone, in the dark, being given only salt foods and no water. Maybe kept bound or chained too. Those things weren't classed as torture, they were just part of the softening-up process. Then there was all the stuff you read about in the spy novels. Sleep deprivation, total isolation, that sort of thing.'

He paused long enough to rearrange Anna's feet, then went on, 'And you'd be watched, to see if the devil came for you.'

'I don't get you,' Anna said.

Simon laughed, reached out a hand to rumple Anna's smooth black hair. 'Well, for instance, you'd been accused of witchcraft, right? You find yourself bound hand and foot to a stool and sitting right in the middle of a cell, knowing that your accusers were watching everything that happened through a peephole in the wall. The belief was that the devil could come to his servant in any guise he chose. A rat, maybe, even a spider. If the watchers saw anything of that kind enter the cell, well, that would be it. Conclusive proof that they'd got it right. That the accusation was valid and it was time to get the ropes ready.'

Anna was incredulous. 'You're kidding us.'

'No, 'fraid not. It was no joke either to the accuser or the accused. Witchcraft had come to be seen as the Devil's work. Once accused, well, you were as good as dead.'

'I remember reading somewhere,' Fergus said slowly, 'that the lives lost between about sixteen-twenty and seventeen-thirty could be counted in their millions.'

Simon nodded. 'It's impossible to know. Head counts have been done, but this was a time of such religious and political turmoil throughout Europe, and so much of the evidence is corrupt. Estimates vary. Some claim tens of thousands, others millions. I don't suppose we'll ever know for sure.'

Cassie's mind was beginning to wander. With half an ear she heard Simon telling them about nature religion at the heart of the modern witch cult, as it had been in the past. Of how it was an expression of the duality of nature, and of people, worshipping a twinned male and female image as a symbol of the God-force. She heard Anna comment that the worship of mother earth in any form was probably a positive step if it brought awareness of environmental problems. She heard the talk veer full circle, to stand once more on Tan's hill and Simon's speculations that in earlier times it had probably figured in local beliefs as a place where the world of man and the world of spirit-beings met. A doorway into another world.

'Fairyland!' Anna's voice was contemptuous.

'Well, something like that.' Simon's voice showed

both amusement and vague insult at Anna's laughter.

'Maybe that's where Suzie went.' The words, spoken with an attempt at flippancy, were out before she had a chance to recall them.

'Cousin Suzie?' Simon was quick to challenge.

Cassie hesitated, found she was beyond returning. 'She disappeared. No one knows what happened or where she went to. She disappeared on the Greenway and that was it. She was gone. I was left behind.'

For several long moments no one spoke. Cassie felt Fergus's arm tighten around her and heard his voice, calm and reassuring. 'That's why we've come here,' he said. 'Cassie needed to be able to face this place again.'

It was some time before anyone said anything sensible. Simon, temporarily at a loss, made polite noises, while Anna, with her usual calm practicality, made tea and gave Cassie space in which to collect her thoughts.

Then, as she placed the tea tray upon the low table close to where they sat, she said, 'You may as well go on now, love. You've made a start, do yourself a favour and get it over with.'

She handed Cassie her tea and sat down once more beside Simon, watching Cassie's slow, acquiescent nod.

'There's not much to tell, really,' Cassie said, trying belatedly to play down the drama of her partial revelation. 'Like I said, Suzie went missing. I guess it happens all the time.'

She sipped her tea, scalding her tongue. 'I used to stay here in the holidays. I've told you that already. Aunty Pat is my mother's sister, but they're very different, she was always really relaxed, easy going. I felt more a part of her family than I did my own.' She paused, uncertain again.

Anna prompted. 'Was Suzie about your age?'

'Two years older. When she went missing, she'd just celebrated her twelfth birthday. Here, it wasn't like it was at home. Provided we said when we'd be back, where we were going, that sort of thing, we could do pretty much what we liked. Everyone knew Pat and her family, and you couldn't go very far without someone noticing. We were allowed to go to the beach on our own provided we didn't swim, and that's what we'd done that day.'

'The day she'd disappeared?'

'Yes. Twenty-fifth August. It had been really hot.' Not a date she would ever forget. 'We'd lazed around on the beach and then watched some of Aunty Pat's neighbours bring their catch in. They'd been collecting the lobster traps. We'd forgotten the time and when we left the beach we were already late. Suzie wasn't worried, it was only a matter of ten minutes or so and Aunty Pat always told us to be back around twenty minutes before she actually expected us, just to make sure we got there on time. But I was worried. I hated being late for anything.' She smiled wryly. 'I still do. Part of my mother's legacy, I suppose. But the thing is, I can't help thinking, if we'd gone the long way round by the road, instead of trying to make up time taking the short cut along the Greenway, I can't help asking myself if Suzie would still be here.'

Cassie fell silent, staring at her tea as though she might find answers in the cooling liquid.

'Go on,' Fergus said gently. 'You're doing fine.'

She managed to award him a rather watery smile, and continued.

'We'd cut along the Greenway before, and this time should have been the same. We turned off the road and were running down the path when suddenly . . . suddenly everything went strange. It was as if the whole world shifted out of focus for an instant and then everything went black. For some reason, I must have lost consciousness and when I came round, I was alone. There was no sign of Suzie.'

Cassie hesitated again. Her chest felt tight and the familiar panic had begun to close in again. She reached out for Fergus's hand, forcing her thoughts into some kind of proper shape before carrying on.

'I remember being scared, confused. At first I didn't even know where I was or what was going on. Then I remembered that Suzie should be with me and she wasn't. I started to shout, calling her name over and over again. But she'd gone.'

Cassie tailed off, unable to keep the mournful note from her voice. How could she tell them that the worst thing was not that Suzie had gone – and even then, she had somehow known the absence was a final one – but the knowledge that Suzie had been taken and she had been left behind? Rejected.

Anna was reaching across, trying to offer comfort; Simon, frowning slightly, as he did when he was

21

considering all possible answers and appropriate responses. Fergus did what she needed most. He held her tight, his silent sympathy helping her to regain control.

'I heard them calling,' she said. 'When we'd not come back Aunty Pat had come looking for us and when she couldn't find us she'd got the neighbours in to help. I heard them calling to us and shouted back. I still didn't know what had happened, I just knew that when I woke up, Suzie was gone.'

The words continued to flow. Cassie, wrapped in memory, recalled how her aunt, frantic with worry, had shaken her. Had shouted at her, begging to know what had happened to her daughter. How she had wanted desperately for someone to cuddle her close, tell her that everything was going to be all right; that Suzie was safe at home and she needn't worry any more. She wanted so much for her aunt to stop shouting at her. Stop asking her questions she had no answers for and all the other faces, other voices, crowding in on her, anxious and demanding until someone pushed them all aside and lifted the child Cassie, carried her to where it was quiet and there was stillness and darkness to hide in. Sleep. Forgetfulness. Retreat. Peace.

'My parents came down that night, wanting to take me home. I can remember my mother and Aunty Pat arguing and Uncle Mike shouting at them both to be quiet. I knew my mother blamed my aunt for letting us run wild. Have too much of our own way. I knew as well that Aunty Pat blamed me. She couldn't help herself. People need someone or something to blame when they're hurt and I was just the closest thing. She kept saying over and over again, why my girl? Why did they take my Suzie? I knew she'd rather I'd been the one to disappear . . . she couldn't help it . . . it just hurt her so much.'

Tears came, inevitably, dripping into the remains of her tea. She clasped both hands around the mug, her shoulders tense, muscles clenched tight along the length of her back.

She heard Anna's voice, angry and defensive, telling her that it wasn't her fault. That no one could possibly blame her for what had happened to Suzie. Simon's questions, unemotional, flatly investigative as they always were when he wished to distance himself from anything that evoked strong feelings. Fergus answering for her.

'They never found out. The last person to see the girls was a woman hanging out washing in one of the cottage gardens facing the main road. She said she saw them running, headed out of the village, but had assumed at the time that they'd continued along the main road. The first search was made along their normal route, the roadway loops back and then turns towards the estate you could see from the hill today.'

Simon nodded. He said, 'How long had they been missing by then?'

It was Cassie who answered, suddenly finding refuge in Simon's unemotional questioning. 'It was about an hour and a half after we should have been back by the time they found me.'

'And they never found Suzie?'

Cassie shook her head. 'No. There was no trace. The police questioned me, questioned everyone. They searched. I mean the search went on for weeks. But there was nothing. Ever.' She paused, looking up at Simon. 'People said all sorts of things. That she'd been murdered, kidnapped. Even that she'd run away. I mean, why would Suzie ever want to run away? I think that must have hurt her parents most of all, that people could think she wanted to run away.'

'And you. What happened to you? Did you fall, hit your head? Did you faint? Did you ever have fits, you know, epilepsy, something like that? Maybe Suzie got scared, ran to get help and someone snatched her.'

Simon was speculating wildly.

Cassie smiled slightly and shook her head. 'It's all been thought of. I didn't have anything like that, the doctors even ran tests just to make sure. In the end they said I must have tripped, maybe hit a stone and knocked myself out. Only problem with that theory was, there was no bruise. No one knows what happened, not to either of us.'

She paused, then continued more slowly. 'My mum and dad took me home. The police came several times to ask questions but I could tell them nothing. In the end they gave up. Closed the file or whatever it is they do. We hardly saw Aunty Pat after that. They held a memorial service in the village church on the first

24

anniversary. Pat had gotten so much older. I went with my parents, but they wouldn't let me talk to her, not that I was talking to anyone really. The doctors said it was shock. That I'd sort of withdrawn. Even then, I knew Pat still thought it was my fault. She wished it was my memorial they were attending and not Suzie's.'

There seemed little more to say after that. Operating on automatic, Cassie rinsed the mugs while Anna made more tea. She could hear Simon, continuing to question the why's and wherefore's of the situation. Trying to find some new angle.

Cassie had heard them all so many times.

Somehow, the fact that Simon, a real know-all in the nicest possible way, should be as baffled as the families, the village and the police had been back then was reassuring. It made her feel less helpless. Less stupid.

Impulsively, she crossed to where her coat was hanging behind the kitchen door and withdrew from the pocket the much folded paper in its protective wrapping.

'This was Suzie,' she said, unfolding the page carefully and laying it on the floor at their feet. She could feel Fergus's reproach.

'I thought I'd got rid of all that,' he said.

She shook her head. 'There's just this. It wasn't one of the things Mum had.'

Fergus frowned, remembering the pile of newspaper clippings and the like that Cassie's mother had kept, not for the sake of remembrance, but to constantly

warn her daughter of what happened to children whose
parents were more liberal – or, as she saw it, more lax
– than she was herself. Cassie's mother had believed
in keeping her daughter's rope tight, especially after
Cassie's father had left them. Fergus had made a bonfire
of the clippings one day when Cassie's mother had
been absent. Had confronted her with the ashes on her
return and been ordered from the house. He had gone,
taking Cassie with him. They had never been back.

'Why did you keep this one?' he asked gently. 'I
thought we'd settled all that.'

Cassie bit her lip, shook her head. 'I told you. This
wasn't one of the things my mother had. I kept it, to
remind me . . .'

'More guilt feelings?' His voice a little harder now.
It angered him so much that she'd spent so many years
paying for something that was not her fault.

Simon and Anna were staring at him, not really sure
what the controversy was about. Simon bent to pick
up the paper, look at the time-worn image of a little
girl with a pretty rounded face and straight fair hair
just sweeping her shoulders. He glanced at Cassie, at
her delicate, rather fragile features, slightly angular
chin. Soft grey eyes, a full, expressive mouth and an
often untidy tangle of brown curls gave her an overall
prettiness. Not beautiful like his Anna, with her dark
eyes and soft black hair cut into a shining bob. No, not
beautiful, but still arresting.

'Not much alike to look at, were you?'

It was such an irrelevant comment, said in such an

indignant tone that it somehow broke the tension. Cassie found herself laughing.

Anna gave her a worried look. 'Are you all right?' she said anxiously. 'Simon, that was thoughtless even for you.'

Cassie was laughing helplessly, trying very hard to regain control. Anna was staring at her. Her outraged expression only serving to add to her inappropriate and now choking giggles. She fought to regain some degree of composure.

'Yes, yes, I'm fine. I'm sorry, it's just that suddenly . . .' She trailed off, unable to explain, unable almost to draw breath.

Anna looked at Fergus, her eyes confused, a little hurt.

'She'll be fine in a moment or two,' he said. Anna saw that he was smiling too. She shrugged. It was in Anna's nature to be fiercely loyal to those she counted friends and if Cassie wanted to laugh hysterically at the wrong moment, well, that was just the way of things.

As always, when confused, Anna took refuge in action, began to clear away the last of the crockery, tidy the small kitchen for the night. By the time she had returned to her seat, Cassie had regained control of herself. Simon had gone to rummage in the kitchen drawer for matches and the whole atmosphere had changed to one of charged solemnity.

Simon handed the matches to Fergus. He shook his head.

27

'No, this is for Cassie to do,' he said.

Cassie's hand was shaking as she lit the match, placed the flame against the edge of the yellowed paper and watched it catch. She held the paper until it came too close to her fingers for her to bear the heat any longer, then dropped it into the empty grate, watched as the final corner was consumed by the creeping flame. Poking lightly with her fingers at the burnt paper, she broke the whole into indistinguishable fragments of ash. Sighing deeply, she sat back on her heels.

Could she let go now? No. Nothing was that easy, but, as Fergus was so fond of saying, this was just one more step. One more thing to cross off the list.

She looked up at him and smiled, enjoying the way his eyes crinkled into ready-made lines when he smiled at her.

Anna was looking curiously at her, but she smiled too, and bent to kiss the top of Cassie's head.

'It's been a long day,' she said, and, taking Simon by the hand, she led him off upstairs to bed.

For a little longer Cassie sat on the worn rug, staring into the black grate.

'Come on, now.' Fergus held out his hand to her. 'When did I last tell you that I loved you?'

He pulled Cassie to her feet, wrapped his arms tightly around her.

'Don't tell me,' she said quietly. 'Show me.'

Chapter Three

Fergus watched Cassie paddling like a child in the shallow water. She looked content, peaceful. The slight breeze lifted her hair, tumbling the dark curls into disarray, and when she turned to smile at him her eyes sparkled. Beautiful, he thought. Really beautiful. The day was still bright, warm too, but a darker grey band running close to the horizon promised change. In the hour they had already spent on the beach, the wind had freshened, veered from the west, and Fergus imagined that he could already taste the rain.

He sighed peaceably. The last few days had been about as perfect as they could get. The company of friends, the exploration of a fascinating, history-soaked county, and, best of all, the late evenings, that private time filled with loving, sharing pleasure with his Cassie. He had to smile at himself, remembering the fierce, possessive joy he took afterwards in watching her sleep.

He had been so fearful of bringing her here, knowing that it had to be faced, terrified of the possible consequences. Looking at her now, he could not help but feel vindicated. Not just for bringing her back here, but believing for the last five years that Cassie could break free of the suffocating cocoon of self-doubt, wrapped tight around her by memories of childhood. This was his Cassie. The one he glimpsed tantalizingly, behind the fear, the self-doubt, the waking nightmare. To say that he loved her would be like saying that he needed to breathe. Sometimes, it worried him, knowing that his passion for her was just as obsessive in its own way as anything Cassie's mother had been able to contrive. He told himself, this is a healthy feeling, life-enhancing – not something that damns the soul.

She had turned and was walking back up the beach towards him. He reached for her, held her close, savouring her warmth, the scent of her, the way her body moved against his, curving against him, as though completing a pattern.

'I love you, so much.' She spoke softly, leaning close for a moment, then turning in his arms to look out to sea once more. 'You were so right, I should have done this years ago.' She spoke quietly. Her words happy, emphatic.

Fergus laughed, hugged her closer. 'Glad you didn't,' he said. 'If you had, I might not have been here with you.'

'Selfish, eh!'

'You bet on it.'

They stood in silence, then Cassie moved suddenly. 'We should be heading back, we promised to be back at the cottage for breakfast, and you know what Simon's like about getting the day planned out.'

Fergus laughed. 'Down to the last detail,' he said.

They turned, walked, hands clasped, back up the beach to the place where the sandy footpath fed its way through an unexpected dip in the cliff face.

'Your walk last night—' Fergus began.

'Helped me sort a lot of things out. I proved to myself that I could go back there, on my own and walk the full length.'

'You went down onto the Greenway?' Fergus sounded almost startled.

She nodded. 'It seemed like the right thing to do.' She half laughed. 'You know, it was all so . . . normal. Almost an anti-climax really. I'd been scared all these years, and then, when I actually got the courage to go and face my demons, I found they were as dead as those poor witches Simon was talking about the other night. Nothing there. Memories, but nothing that couldn't be firmly put in its place.'

She spoke positively, confidently, but Fergus could not help but cast an anxious glance at her. He'd seen her before like this, each step forward had brought on this kind of euphoria, this delight in living. He loved to see her so happy, rejoicing in strengths so hard won, but experience told him that the highs never lasted. These things did even out though, he reminded himself. Her mood swings were far less extreme now than they had been, her problems more often solved by their own joint efforts.

She looked at him, her glance half-amused, half-exasperated and clasped his hand more tightly.

'And you can stop looking at me like that, Fergus

Maltham,' she said, laughing out loud as he began to protest his innocence.

She threw her arms around him, still laughing, and Fergus clung to her as though that way he could hold the moment for ever. Keep life always this perfect. He had fought so hard to get her this far, believed in her . . . needed her. She snuggled against him, her warm body soft against him.

'We'll be all right, Fergus. Everything will be all right now.'

Anna breathed deeply. The air was fresh, slightly chilled by the sea breeze and the day, for the moment, bright blue and promising sunshine. 'Which means it will probably rain before midday,' she thought wryly.

She began to stroll lazily towards the village. They would need more milk for breakfast, and she wanted the morning papers, but there was no hurry. Simon was still debating whether or not to get out of bed and Cassie and Fergus would be unlikely to be back yet. Anna welcomed the brief time alone, time to think – though not to any real purpose – and to just enjoy the morning. Much as she loved Simon life with him tended to be – when once he had made that final move out of bed – one mad flight from project to project, destination to destination. Simon tended to view travelling time, whether literal or not, to be the source of wasted energy and frustration whereas Anna sometimes welcomed the opportunity to enjoy the trip.

This particular trip was not a long one. Seven minutes each way according to Simon. Anna managed to make it last fifteen. The shop bell rang and she called a greeting to the woman emerging from the back. This morning walk had become a regular feature and she had struck up quite a rapport with the locals. That was Anna's way. Her open acceptance of people tended to bring rewards. She chatted amiably to the woman while collecting the few purchases she needed and turned to place them on the counter. The woman already had the papers ready for her. Two of the big nationals and the local daily. Anna paid, glancing casually at the papers as she waited for her change.

What she saw made her stiffen, her body reacting in panic even before she could get the words out. 'Oh, my God.'

The woman looked across at her, then down at the paper. 'Yes, dear. Just terrible isn't it. The poor parents, they're going frantic. Had half the village out last night they did and again this morning. They knocked at the cottage, figured you might want to help out, but there was no one there.'

Anna stared blankly at her, then managed, 'No, we went out till late. Oh, but this is dreadful.'

The woman nodded. 'Like I said love, they've had people out searching this morning, too. I'm surprised you didn't see them, but then you wouldn't, not walking the route the way you do.'

She looked expectantly for a response, and Anna managed something she hoped was appropriate. The

33

woman continued, telling her that the police had been up at the Top Farm all night. 'Doing house-to-house this morning, I shouldn't wonder.'

Anna managed to nod, to string something appropriately sensible together, but she could barely take her eyes from the image on the front of the local paper. She accepted her change automatically, assured the woman that if they could be of any help . . . and managed to push bread and milk into her bag. Hands clutched sweatily at the paper and she managed to fumble the shop door open. Then she ran, panic turning her stomach to water, sight hazed by tears. Anna ran and didn't stop running until the cottage door had been thrown open and an astonished Simon was confronted by the front-page image of a blonde-haired, smiling child, pretty round face framed by hair that just skimmed her shoulders.

Simon stared, then picked up the paper and began to read aloud.

'Sara Jane Cassidy, aged ten, missing since yesterday afternoon.' He continued to read, his voice dropping as he related, more to himself now than to Anna, the circumstances surrounding the child's disappearance. Anna's mind caught only those things that she already knew. Last night. The Greenway. A little girl who looked like Suzanne Ashmore.

'Oh, my God,' she whispered softly. 'Cassie.'

Chapter Four

Detective Inspector Tynan – retired – was about to sit down to breakfast when the early-morning paper spilled onto the doormat. He scooped it up and hurried through to the kitchen, attempting to catch the kettle before its low whistle cursed into an exaggerated shriek. Every morning he told himself that he should invest in an electric one. A nice, quiet, automatically switch-offable one; but he never did. Instead he indulged each day in the game of seeing just how much of his essential housework he could get done before the kettle became deafeningly insistent. It caused him some wry amusement, when he actually gave it thought, that he, after years of taxing his skills and measuring his time and endurance against the minds and skills of other people, should now be reduced to competing with a whistling kettle.

He had filled the teapot and set about buttering his toast before he actually got around to looking at the paper. What he saw struck him cold, knife paused in mid-stroke. He put down both knife and toast and gave the paper his full concentration. A ten-year-old – playing with her friends one minute, gone the next. It was the where of it, that and the burning familiarity of the image that gave him pause. The Greenway. That lonely, high-hedged bit of pathway that seemed designed to go nowhere. He remembered all right. Remembered too the photograph of another little girl, very like this one, the same mischievous grin on her face. For several minutes, he sat gazing into the past. The image of young Suzie Ashmore transposing itself on to the girl's image in the paper.

Resolutely, he shook himself. Reminded himself that he was retired now and that the other case had been close on twenty years before. He turned the page deliberately, picked up the knife and continued with his buttering, forcing himself to take an interest in the reports of local fêtes and the doings of minor dignitaries. It wasn't working. He swore as the over-cooked and overcold toast fragmented when he bit into it and reminded himself, again, that he was retired. This was nothing to do with him. Should there be any connection between the two cases then they knew where to find him.

Gloomily, he reached across to pour the tea. His right hand thus occupied, he allowed his left, almost surreptitiously, to turn the paper back to the front page, his eyes moving from the other minor stories, scattered as space fillers, back to the face of Sara Jane Cassidy. He began to read again, giving up now on all appearance of indifference. Who was heading the case? No, it would be too early for that to be in the report and most likely the child would turn up sometime today anyway and the whole thing would all be over.

Even as he thought that, he dismissed it. No. There were few places she could have gone to. The report said that her friends were playing at the entrance to the Greenway, so any abduction by car would have taken them first, not Sara Jane. She was too far from the sea for there to have been danger of drowning or of a fall from the cliff. To have accomplished that, the child would have had to have gone back through the village, not further inland up the pathway. He shook his head. There were too many damned similarities.

Tynan got up, headed for the hall and the phone. Retired he might be, but certainly not senile, even if he did race kettles for exercise these days. Feeling more alive than he had done in months, and knowing a pang of guilt that it was the disappearance, perhaps worse, of a little girl that had made him feel this way, Tynan picked up the phone and began to dial.

Chapter Five

Mike Croft pushed himself back to standing and shrugged his shoulders to ease the tension. His poking around at ground level had told him little he did not already know; grass bruised by children's feet skidding across its surface, sand and shells from an overturned plastic bucket shaped like a miniature castle, and the ball they had played with left abandoned on the grass when they had first noted that Sara Jane was missing.

The children, six of them – the youngest eight, the eldest almost fifteen. He'd talked to them all this morning, a small frightened cluster, red-eyed and over-awed, gathered with their parents in the village hall. He'd let them tell their story as a group, and pieced the afternoon together. Had drawn out, little by little the trivia of beach games, their walk back through the village and the game they had played at the entrance to the Greenway, kicking the ball backwards and forwards across the narrow road.

He glanced around him, standing with his back to the Greenway, facing the road. That had been around four p.m. They could be fairly certain of the time as three of the six had worn watches; all had to be home at around five.

The short walk back into the village would have taken no more than five minutes, allow ten for the youngest two who lived the far end to be escorted to their door. Jenny Wilding, the eldest child, had said that it had been about four-forty when she had begun to warn them they'd soon have to head back. It was then that they realized Sara Jane was no longer with them.

Mike thought back to the earlier interview. He really felt for the girl. Jenny apparently had a reputation for reliability. She was taking Sara's disappearance personally.

'I did watch them,' she had insisted. 'Three of the younger ones, Sara, Beth and Jo, they'd got tired and didn't want to play so they sat down to look at Bethie's shells.' He remembered how she'd glanced around her then, looking for support from the others. Tony, the second eldest, had spoken up for her.

'You can't blame Jenny.' The declaration belligerent. 'We did watch them and they seemed OK. You know, messing around in the gap and then later running in and out of the Greenway.'

'We asked them if they wanted to join in the game,' Jenny continued. 'You know, they'd perked up a bit by then.' She paused, close to tears. 'They said they were playing their own game and I heard Bethie counting like they were playing hide and seek. I remember thinking it was a daft game to play just there.' Again, she glanced around, looking for confirmation. 'I mean, where's there to hide?' Her voice trailed off and she fumbled in her pocket for an already well-used tissue.

'That's what we thought she was doing.' Tony picked up for Jenny. 'When she didn't come back, I mean. We thought she was just hiding.' He too gave up. He was of an age to not even consider the possibility of tears, but his shoulders slumped and it was evident to Mike that both Jenny and the boy had spent the night thinking of all the things they could have done to keep a closer eye on Sara Jane.

'And when you couldn't find her and she didn't come back?' He knew the answer from last night's interviews, but still . . .

'We got scared.' It was Beth who replied this time. 'Jenny said Sara might be hurt or something and we should get help. We was late then too. I thought my mum would be mad.'

'So you went back to the village?'

Beth nodded. 'Tom and Jo stayed behind just in case she really was hiding and thought we'd all gone and left her.'

'And who thought of that?' Mike asked gently.

'Jenny did.'

Mike smiled at the child, gave Jenny an approving nod. 'Well, I think that was very sensible of her, don't you?'

He'd let them go then. Parents had stayed to speak to him, bewildered, angry. He had felt the entire pressure of this close-knit community bearing down on him. One of theirs was missing. Just what was he going to do about it?

He sighed.

If it hadn't been for Jenny, insisting that the two boys remain behind, he would have assumed abduction. That the little girl had been hiding, hoping to scare her friends maybe and let the joke go too far, been snatched as she came back onto the main road. That in itself would have been coincidence piled on coincidence, but it would have made a kind of sense, given him somewhere to start. As it was . . .

'Sir?'

Sergeant Enfield's voice cut through his thoughts. He turned towards him. 'Yes, Bill?'

The other man relaxed, smiled slightly. 'We've had a phone call.'

'I imagine we've had a lot of those.'

Bill Enfield allowed himself the luxury of a full smile this time. 'More than a few,' he acknowledged, 'but this one might be useful.'

'Oh.'

'You ever get to meet DI Tynan? Held your job before Flint.'

Mike shook his head. 'No, we never got to meet. Why?'

'Well, that's who the call was from. Offers his services he does, should you want them.'

Mike cast the older man a puzzled look. By tacit consent they had begun to walk back to the village and the incident room set up in the village hall.

'I get the feeling you think I should accept,' he said.

'Could do worse.'

41

There was a pause. Mike had held his post here for a few months only. Long enough though to get to know the regional officers like Bill Enfield. Long enough to know that Bill was best telling things his own way. He waited as the older man prepared himself.

'Tynan investigated a similar case. A child, gone missing, playing on the Greenway. Name of—'

'Ashmore. Suzanne Ashmore. Sorry, Bill, the jungle drums got in ahead of you.'

'We don't have no jungle drums here, boy, we beat our own rhythm out on the boat keels.' He smiled quickly at Mike. There had been liking between them right from when Mike had first joined Divisional. Not like his predecessor. Flint was a by-the-book man. This one had respect for local knowledge, local people, men like himself, doing the same job year in year out.

'But since you know so much you'll know that Suzie Ashmore was never found.' He paused before continuing. 'First big case Tynan ever handled that was and it rankled with him all through that he couldn't solve it.' He paused again, looked sideways at Mike. 'I told them at control to pass on he'd be welcome. Sir.' This last a gentle reminder that they'd reached the first houses.

'All right, Sergeant. If ex-DI Tynan feels he has something to say then I'll listen. But dammit, Enfield, that was what, fifteen years ago?'

'More like twenty, sir.'

'Coincidence, has to be.' He shrugged, suddenly angry. What else could it be? He felt too a moment of irritation towards Enfield. Bill Enfield thought he needed a handholder, did he? He squashed the thought almost as it arrived. If Bill Enfield had a moment of doubt on that score, Mike would know it by now. Lower rank he might be, but round here it was experience, local knowledge that counted. Flint, Mike's predecessor had fallen flat on his face by ignoring that, had practically sunk without trace in the cow shit.

He sighed, grimaced slightly and spoke. 'We'd better talk to the parents again.'

Cassie had taken the news better than Anna had hoped. She read the report carefully, face pale and drawn, but seemed calm, concerned only for the child.

'I should tell them I was there,' she said.

'When?' Anna questioned.

'Last night, well, evening really. Six, six-thirty, you remember, I went for a walk just before we drove out to Norwich.'

'You went there, to the Greenway, on your own? Did you see them, the children I mean? No. I guess they would have gone by then.' She frowned. 'The woman in the shop, she said they were searching. Didn't you see anyone?'

Cassie shook her head thoughtfully. 'There was no one on the Greenway, not then. But if they were searching for her they'd surely have moved further out by then. There's not that much of the Greenway to search.'

Fergus, standing behind her, placed hands gently on Cassie's shoulders.

'Well,' he said, 'we should let someone know. You might have seen something, without knowing it, I mean.' He broke off, hands moving gently to massage his wife's shoulders. He could feel the tension in them, feel her shaking. He cursed silently. Why this? Why now? It ruined everything. Then he felt overwhelmed by guilt as he thought of the child, wherever she was. Dead maybe, or alive and frightened. Of her parents. His hands tightened on Cassie as the questions in his head repeated themselves, just to spite him. Why this? Why now?

'They've set up an incident room,' Simon said. 'We talked to the Thorsons at the shop, found out what we could. Said if they needed extra help with anything . . .'

Fergus nodded. 'Of course,' he said. This tragedy was theirs as well, he thought. For good or ill they were involved.

Suddenly, he felt completely overwhelmed. The peace, the optimism of only an hour or so ago evaporating like sea mist, the resentment he felt as unbearable as it was unfair. He swallowed nervously, feeling very selfish, tears pricking at the corners of his eyes, felt Cassie's shoulders begin to shake more violently as if his own grief communicated to her through his touch.

'Cassie. Love.'

She seemed to collapse forward out of his partial embrace, head dropping, burying her face in her arms resting on the tabletop.

'Cassie!'

Fergus reached out for her again, only to be distracted by a sharp rap on the outer door. Reluctantly, Anna went to open it. She returned a few moments later, a young constable in tow.

'It's the police,' she said irrelevantly. 'They're doing house-to-house, want to ask some questions.'

The officer glanced at her, then allowed his gaze to travel over the others in the room, finally resting on Cassie, her head raised now, trying to regain some measure of control.

'Are you all right, Miss?' he asked.

Mike allowed the local man to precede him into the Cassidys' sitting room, detaining the WPC in the hallway. The young woman looked pale and tired, well into overtime now and feeling the strain. He didn't envy her. Close, undiluted proximity to grief was worse, far worse than a night of activity. Hard work could be remedied by a hot bath and a night's sleep. The kind of watching, supporting role she had been playing only sapped the mind.

'How are they coping?' It was, he knew, a silly question.

She gave him a wry, somewhat crooked smile. 'Stopped raging and started crying at around two, sir. Doctor came and gave Janice, Mrs Cassidy, a sedative, so she's had a bit of sleep. Mr's spent the night pacing. Keeps going to the garden gate, watching for her.' She sighed. 'Any more news, sir?'

He shook his head. 'Nothing yet. We'll see what

house-to-house turns up, take it from there.' He gave her a sympathetic look. 'I'll get someone in to relieve you, soon as we can.'

From the sitting room he could hear Bill Enfield's voice, low and calm as ever, the modulated burr of it designed to sooth. Too much to hope it would work now. He could hear Mrs Cassidy, voice high and plaintive, words broken and her husband, angry, bewildered. He turned to enter the room. 'Go down and get yourself fed,' he told the WPC. She smiled, thanked him and disappeared with almost inhuman haste.

Sighing, Mike entered the room.

Janice Cassidy was seated on a small blue sofa, husband beside her. She was, he guessed in her early thirties, but right now she could have been anything up to fifty. Short blonde hair that should have stood in slightly spiky waves, sagged above a pleasantly high forehead softened by a sparse fringe. Wet blue eyes, red-rimmed. It was easy to see where Sara Jane had got her prettiness. Her slight tendency towards plumpness too. The father was dark, tall, heavily built. His dark eyes as red-rimmed as his wife's.

'Well?' Cassidy demanded.

Mike waited before answering, sat down opposite them and leaned forward slightly as he began to talk. 'Right now, I don't have any answers, Mr Cassidy. But . . . please, Mr Cassidy, if you'll let me finish.' He deliberately allowed his voice to rise a little, to allow a note of hardness to creep in. All night these people had endured sympathy, soft reassurances. Now, he suspected, that was the last thing they needed. They wanted action, someone who at least gave the appearance of being in control.

Cassidy had fallen silent, surprised at the change in tone. He glared, seemed about to start again so Mike spoke quickly.

'Right now, I can't tell you anything you don't already know. We need answers just as much as you do. We're drafting in every extra officer the Force can supply. The incident room's set up and we're conducting house-to-house, we'll know more when those interviews are complete.' He hoped.

Cassidy had begun to protest again. 'We should be out looking. Not sitting here on our bums doing fuck all.'

'Please, Jim.' His wife laid her hand on his arm.

'We should be though. She could be hurt, could be anywhere.'

Mrs Cassidy bit her lip hard as tears threatened again, her husband circling an arm around her shoulders.

'Should be out looking for her,' he repeated, but some of the fight had gone now.

Mike relaxed a little, knowing that he was getting through. 'If you feel up to it you can join the search later.' He felt Bill Enfield's eyes on him, disapproving, but continued anyway. 'We'll be asking for volunteers, anyone who can spare an hour or so.'

Cassidy nodded. For the first time there was a slight relaxation of the muscles at the corners of his mouth.

'We'll need you to help liaise between the different groups.' He felt Bill ease off on him. Liaison, well that was different from actually putting the parents in the front line where they might find . . . well, he'd rather not think that far.

'We'll need you with us, need to know everything we can about where Sara likes to play, her hiding places, the kind of games she likes, anything that might give us a clue. We know that she ran into the Greenway, we don't know where she might have gone to after that.' He paused, hesitated for a moment, then said, 'Tell me about her, what's she like? A loner or someone who wants to be in a group?' He paused again, then smiled encouragingly. The Cassidys exchanged a quick look, not knowing where to begin, but, it seemed, glad to be at least involved in something. Mrs Cassidy tried to speak, then closed her mouth again, suddenly, as though clamping down on threatened tears. Mike could feel the whole scenario threatening to collapse and prepared another tack. It was Bill Enfield who rescued him, getting to his feet and smiling at Janice Cassidy. 'Maybe I could help you make some tea, my dear,' he suggested, opening the living-room door and waiting for her to move. She rose gratefully, finding refuge in the ordinary, the practical, in Bill Enfield's quiet authority.

Mike waited until they had gone, glancing around the room before speaking. Cassidy got in first, asking the question uppermost in his mind.

'You think she's dead?' He asked it brusquely, with

artificial calm. He might have been asking for a judgement on the day's weather.

For a moment, Mike weighed platitudes. Then shook his head. 'I don't want to think that, Mr Cassidy. None of us do.'

Cassidy stared at him as though hoping for more. Then he sighed, leaned back in his seat, closing his eyes.

'Jim,' he said, 'might as well call me Jim.' He shook himself as though it would help to clear his head. Mike sensed he wanted time to get his thoughts in order, glanced around the room again.

'You're a farm worker.'

'Yes, foreman up at Top Farm.'

Mike nodded. The room was comfortable. Two matching sofas, blue moquette. They looked new. Then the chair he was sitting in. Old, scuffed and faded-green leather with a peculiar studded pattern on the face of both arms.

The curtains had a newish look to them, bought maybe to go with the sofas. The carpet, older, had begun to fade.

There were photos and cheap prints everywhere. The photos, many of them featuring Sara Jane, had the look of family snapshots, taken by a competent amateur. The prints the kind that Mike's wife had been fond of. The kind of thing that could be seen everywhere.

Sara Jane was an only child.

Why did that make it worse?

Cassidy was speaking again. Voice low, controlled.

'The boss called earlier, said you was to have any men you needed. Nothing much'll get done today I reckon.' He stopped again, looking Mike in the eyes.

'Round here, we don't expect these things to happen. Not here.' He leaned forward. Mike could already guess what he was about to hear, knew the man had to say it and got his official protest at the ready.

'You hear me, Mr Detective Inspector Croft, you just listen. You'd better find her and you'd better find the bastard that took her away. For his sake, Mr Detective Inspector, you'd better pray for his sake that you get to him first.'

Chapter Six

Anna gave the constable one of her best 'I'm not feeling intimidated by a mere policeman' smiles and offered him tea. He declined, politely, a little queasily too, Anna thought. No doubt the same offer had been made more than once this morning.

Cassie, more composed now, had turned towards him.

'I'm sorry,' she said. 'I was just upset, the news, it . . . it made me think of things.'

'Miss?'

Fergus took over.

'We were just on our way down to you, Officer. To the incident room that is.'

'Really, sir.' The young man's face took on an air of careful, professional interest. 'Well, any help you feel you can give . . .?'

He left the implied question hanging between them. Fergus sighed. 'It's probably nothing very useful,' he said, trying very hard to give Cassie a breathing space.

The constable waited with polite, but impatient attention. Fergus took the plunge.

'The fact is, my wife was walking in the Greenway at around six last night. I know it's not the time in question, but it's always possible she might have seen something and not realized it. We, well that is—' He broke off, looked at Cassie who sat motionless but seemingly composed. 'The fact is, we thought we should at least report it.'

The Constable nodded slowly. This was not news to him. The searchers out last evening had reported seeing the woman walking in the direction of the Greenway, had called out to her. They said she had waved and walked on, obviously too far distant to hear them.

He glanced once more around the room. There was tension here that ran far deeper than mere distress for a child none of these strangers even knew. He turned his attention back to Cassie.

'If I could just have your name.'

'Cassie, Cassandra Maltham.' She indicated Fergus. 'This is my husband.' Her tone, almost over-controlled, made Fergus think of formal introductions. He reacted to her tone automatically, reached out, almost as though to shake hands, saw the young officer's face and allowed his hand to drop uselessly to his side once more.

The Constable wrote the names down. 'And you were on your own, Mrs Maltham?'

Cassie nodded.

'And about what time was this?'

Cassie wasn't certain. 'Six, six-fifteen, no later.'

'She was back here by six-thirty. We left then to go into Norwich.' Anna had spoken quickly, almost defensively. She fell silent as the officer glanced at her, a slight frown creasing the space between his eyebrows.

'Thank you, Miss,' he said, pointedly, and turned back to Cassie. Anna sighed, sat down at the table opposite her friend.

'So you were back here by six-thirty then?'

Cassie nodded. 'Yes, it couldn't have been any later than that. I really wasn't out for very long, I just needed to walk for a while.'

Her distress was increasing again – she'd chosen the Greenway for her walk – it was impossible to hide it. The Constable frowned again, sensing once more the tension that seemed inconsistent with the scene.

Anna reached across the table, took Cassie's hand. 'It's all right, sweetheart. Just a few questions. There's nothing you can tell them.'

Again the Constable awarded her an impatient glance. 'I think that's for us to decide, Miss, don't you?'

Anna scowled at him, but said nothing. She looked across at Simon. He'd been uncharacteristically silent during the whole interview.

The Constable was about to speak again, fiddling with his personal radio as though debating whether or not to call in. He wasn't sure about this one. The timing was wrong for the woman to be involved, but that didn't stop her from being there earlier. In any event, from the state of her, she knew something.

He got up from the table, moved over towards the window. 'I'm going to call in, Miss, chances are they'll want you down at the incident room to make a proper statement.' He watched her, seeing what effect his words would have. The woman didn't move. He frowned.

Fergus spoke for her. 'Of course, Officer. Anything we can do.'

The Constable nodded, prepared to call in. His thoughts were broken by the harsh sobbing of the woman seated at the table.

'I was there,' she said. 'She disappeared and I was left behind.'

Fergus tightened his grip on Cassie's shoulders, trying to calm her. Anna reached across, anxiously, knowing how the words must sound.

'You were there, Mrs Maltham?' The officer's voice was sharp with surprise and suspicion. He took a step back towards the table. Anna interrupted loudly.

'Cassie, that wasn't now, that was years ago. It's nonsense to think that has any connection with this.'

Until then, Simon had felt nothing but vague annoyance at the whole interview, now, it looked to be turning very unpleasant. Despite that, he found himself casting a wry glance at Anna. Not connected? He remembered Anna's dramatic rush to bring him the news earlier that morning.

He tempered his mood hastily. This was not the moment for even the vaguest of flippancies.

'What other time, Miss . . .?' the Constable was asking.

Anna glared at him, waved her hand in exasperation, then looked back at Cassie, sitting, head bent, staring at the pattern on the tablecloth. Fergus moved, stepped between Cassie and the rest of them, pulling her head against his belly, stroking her hair protectively.

His voice snapped with anger and his normally gentle blue eyes hardened with the coldness of it. 'My wife knows nothing. Just get out of here and leave her alone.'

The policeman didn't move. When he spoke again, his tone changed to one which, he hoped, emphasized the seriousness of the situation, reminding this member of the public that he was an officer of the law, just doing his job.

'Your wife was on the Greenway, sir. If she has anything which might help us then we must know about it.'

Once more Simon had to fight to control the irrational, irresponsible desire to laugh out loud. It was a desire so strong, he almost choked on it . . . then, he looked at Cassie, motionless, frozen now in a time that should have long since passed. Looked at Fergus, who so rarely showed anything but the most damnable calm but who now appeared ready to take on the world, never mind this meagre representative of British law, in order to defend his woman. And Anna. Eyes desperate, bemused, deeply fearful. Suddenly, there seemed not the slightest – even most inappropriate – sense of amusement left in the situation. Simon bit his lip. Looked away.

The policeman was speaking into his radio, evidently feeling the need for reinforcement. Simon moved to stand beside Fergus.

'She's just upset,' he found himself saying. 'This

whole thing, it's brought back memories. Things she thought she'd put behind her.'

The officer looked at him curiously, an official frown creasing his very young features.

'My superiors will be taking over now, sir,' he said. 'I'm sure they'll be very interested in anything you have to say.'

Simon glared at him. Then he sighed, pulled out a chair and sat down beside Cassie, laying a hand gently on her arm.

Tynan stared down the length of the room at the young woman seated at the table, a little knot of others keeping close to her. Cassie Junor, as was. So she was Cassie Maltham now. He'd often thought of her, wondered how her life had turned out when the files had been shelved and their official contact ended. Could she have something to do with this present mystery? It seemed an obvious conclusion. Too obvious. Tynan instinctively disliked the obvious. It took the interest out of things. He sipped at his tea once more, content to watch. After all, he had no official capacity here – as yet – might never have if this new man, Croft, took exception to his being there.

Heavy footsteps echoing on the wooden floor of the village hall-cum-incident room, made him look up as two men entered. One, he knew. Bill Enfield, been around almost as long as Tynan himself. Due for retirement. The other must be Croft. Tynan watched as both men paused to speak to the young constable who had brought Cassie Maltham and her little party of supporters down here. Bill didn't appear to have changed much, but then, he was one of those men who'd been born looking experienced. Tynan continued to sip his tea contentedly, regarded the second man with interest. Mike Croft was tall, well built, but walked with a slight leftward stoop, as though bending to hear what someone had to say. Dark hair, beginning to show grey and a way of moving that suggested he might at any moment take off at a run.

The two men were approaching him now, Bill Enfield extending a hand, making introductions.

'How are you, Bill?'

'I'm well. Yourself?'

Tynan nodded, aware that Croft's attention had moved from them.

'Cassie Junor, as she was when I knew her. Married to the bloke with the beard.' He paused, Mike Croft hadn't looked at him, but the slight, attentive stoop had increased and Tynan knew he had the other's attention. 'Though how the hell he got her away from that mother of hers . . . Devil himself would have thought twice about tackling Mrs Junor.'

Croft glanced at him. 'I'll be frank. Until I heard of the Maltham woman, I couldn't see how there could be any connection with Suzanne Ashmore. I still don't, unless Mrs Maltham was in some way responsible for the child's disappearance, and on the face of it that doesn't seem likely.'

'Oh?'

Croft had turned to accept a mug of tea. Bill answered for him.

'Seems all four of them were out watching the lobster boats come in, in full view of around a dozen people when Sara Jane went missing. So, unless she had an accomplice . . .' Tynan could hear the shrug in his voice.

'But, in spite of that, you now think there may be a connection?' Tynan asked.

Croft sighed, nodded slowly. 'I don't like coincidence. Twenty years and this place is like the grave. Stolen bicycles, the occasional RTA. Nothing. Then, as soon as Cassie Maltham decides to come back here, this happens.' He'd begun to move towards the now restless and expectant group at the far end of the hall. 'I'm not saying she was responsible, not saying that she wasn't, only that it's too much to pass over, her being here both times.'

Bill fell into step beside his superior. Tynan, their silence to the contrary offering him acceptance, brought up the rear.

Chapter Seven

DI Mike Croft had always thought that the term 'fingertip search' was something of a misnomer. His son had always called it an 'eyes-down-poke-it-with-a-stick-search' and, privately, Mike always thought of it in this way. He missed Steven; missed Maggie too, but now was not the right time to start thinking about that. Angrily, he wrenched his thoughts aside and concentrated on his view of the slow-moving ranks of men and women crossing the field.

The Cassidys had been persuaded home, exhaustion and the growing ranks of journalists had been too much for them to cope with. Mike was glad they had gone. The press had been directed to a cordoned area on the main road and he'd left the liaison to Bill Enfield. He knew, though, that he'd have to make some kind of statement soon.

Glancing across the pea field he could see the Thomases, Anna and Simon at the end of a line of searchers. He cast his mind back to the earlier interview with Cassie Maltham. He'd quietly taken her aside from the others, seated her at a corner table and drawn a chair up at right angles to her, consciously creating a private, controlled space. Tynan had seated himself on the other side, and Bill, ever reliable, had kept the situation calm, arranging tea, encouraging the other three to talk about themselves, their jobs, their lives elsewhere and moved them away from the interview area. Fergus had not been happy, but he'd gone along with things. The other two, Mike knew, had been glad of a break in the tension, Bill had no trouble engaging them in conversation.

That had left Mike to deal with Cassie.

She'd been tense, anxious, obviously distressed, but, equally obviously, eager to be helpful. Mike had kept the questions simple, going over her statement about the walk she had taken in the Greenway, what she had seen – nothing – anything she had noticed as she came back onto the road – nothing. Several times she had glanced at Tynan, as though some half-memory of him stirred, but she had not acknowledged him directly until Mike's questions had drawn to an end and he'd asked her if she had anything further to add. She'd turned, looked properly at Tynan, then back at Mike. Something, it seemed, had to shift from her mind first.

'That constable, the one who came to the cottage.'

Mike nodded.

'He must have thought I was crazy, wondered what he'd walked into.'

Mike gave her a thoughtful look, then said, 'It's been explained to him, about your cousin. I'm sure whatever judgement he made has been tempered by that.'

He'd kept his voice deliberately cool, his answer coldly formal, watching her response. She'd bitten her lip, looked uncertainly at him, then turned once more to Tynan.

'Excuse me, but don't I know you?'

Tynan glanced at Mike, then nodded. 'We've met, Cassie.'

His voice filled in the gaps for her. 'You're the policeman that investigated, when Suzie went, you were there then?'

Tynan nodded slowly. 'DI Tynan that was. I'm officially retired now.'

Bewildered, she looked from one to the other. 'But, you're here. I mean, you think there's a connection? A real connection? But that was twenty years ago.'

Croft was about to answer, Tynan was way ahead. 'There are two connections already, Cassie. The place. Two children missing on the Greenway—'

'And me,' she finished for him, her voice dull, tired.

Tynan nodded.

Cassie looked at Mike Croft once more. 'You think I had something to do with it, don't you?' She was keeping her voice deliberately calm, but Mike could hear that the control was brittle.

He replied cautiously. 'Mrs Maltham, I have to investigate every possibility fully. I can't discount a connection. I can't, yet, discount your involvement.' He rose, so did Tynan, Cassie swallowed nervously, then struggled to her feet.

'You intended to stay here for another three days, I understand?'

She nodded.

'Well, for now, keep to your original plans. You needn't restrict your movements, but it would be helpful if you'd check with one of my officers when you leave the village, just let us know where you plan to be.'

She gave him a sharp, angry look and was about to follow it with words, when a commotion at the entrance to the hall distracted everyone. Mike turned, swore softly as he saw the Cassidys enter, accompanied by the young WPC he had spoken with earlier.

Bill Enfield gave him a wry, sideways glance and moved towards the advancing group. Mike got ready, not certain what tack to play. Mrs Cassidy made the decision for him, rushing forward and grabbing Cassie by the arm.

'Did you see her? Did you see who took her?'

Mike shifted quickly to intercept, but Cassie waved him away. He stopped, deciding to run with the confrontation, see what it exposed.

'It's all right,' Cassie was saying. 'It's all right!'

Mike wasn't certain whether she spoke to him or the distraught woman now clinging to both arms. He was aware of Fergus Maltham and the other two hovering behind him, of Mr Cassidy, embarrassed and awkward.

Cassie was speaking to the other woman. 'If I'd seen anything, believe me, I'd tell. I didn't go to the Greenway till about six, too late to see anything.'

'But you were there, that other time. Maybe you saw something then, maybe something you forgot about, maybe it was the same man took my Sara.' She broke off, stared wildly around her, then howled, 'Can't you understand! My little girl's gone! Can't any of you understand that?'

'Oh, God!' Clumsily, Cassie moved clear of the table. Jim Cassidy held his wife's shoulders, trying to draw her away, get her to release the clawlike grip she had now on both Cassie's arms. His own hands were shaking and he was obviously not in a much better state than his wife.

Mike decided now might be a good time to intervene. He signed to the WPC who came forward to join Jim Cassidy's efforts with his wife. Cassie was speaking again.

'If I knew anything. Oh, God! I wish I did.' The mother was crying now, hysteria over, replaced by a harsh sobbing that cut through the silence which had fallen on the rest of the room. It was Cassie who gathered Janice Cassidy into her arms.

Croft frowned, then gave in to the moment, as the two women, both crying now, headed towards the door. Their husbands following, reluctant, awkward, looking like outsiders. Great picture this was going to make for the waiting press, Croft thought cynically as he'd assigned people to give them escort home.

He'd looked across at the silent figure of John Tynan, wondering what memories were flooding the older man's mind just then.

'If we could just have a few words, Inspector?'

Mike turned an enquiring glance towards the

speaker, taking in as he did so the fact that most of the big dailies and at least two of the TV networks had put in an appearance. The speed with which they arrived at any scene had always amazed him. Did they, he wondered, have the equivalent of flying squads on standby? The thought almost amused him.

'There's little I can tell you at the present. I'm sure you can appreciate, everything that can be done is being done.'

He was amazed as always just how smoothly such platitudes slipped off the tongue; amazed too that they still bothered to write them down.

'Inspector, are you linking this to the Ashmore case?'

Mike paused, then said cautiously, 'Not specifically, but of course, we will rule out no line of enquiry.'

'And Suzanne Ashmore was never found, was she, sir?'

'Unfortunately, she was not.'

'Would you deny, Inspector, that there are many similarities?'

'There are similarities, yes, but the thing you must remember is that Suzanne Ashmore disappeared almost twenty years ago.'

'Philip Andrews of the *Chronicle* here, Inspector.'

Mike glanced sideways at him; one of the locals, this, an elderly man with a much younger photographer in tow. Mike vaguely remembered seeing them earlier when they had left the village hall. 'Yes, Mr Andrews?'

'Seems to me you might be hedging, Inspector.'

'In what way, Mr Andrews?' Mike's voice was polite,

cautiously enquiring. A sudden wariness crept into his thoughts.

'About the connection, Inspector. Didn't I recognize DI Tynan earlier? When Mrs Cassidy and the . . . other woman left the hall?'

His voice held an innocence that reinforced Mike's anxiety. There was little sense in denying Tynan's presence.

He said heavily, 'Ex-DI Tynan has been in touch, yes.'

'And the woman, Inspector. The woman with Mrs Cassidy?'

Mike looked sharply at him, but responded calmly. 'What about her, Mr Andrews?' He was painfully aware that they had the undivided attention of the assembly because Philip Andrews, with his local knowledge, was not about to lose the chance to get one over on the big boys.

'Cassandra Junor, as she was back then. Her married name's Maltham, I believe . . . strange that she should come back here now, Inspector.'

Mike decided that he'd had enough. Rumours had been flying all day and he'd been a fool not to think that Tynan, a local after all, should not be recognized, especially by the likes of Philip Andrews.

Mike was painfully aware that dealing with the press had never been one of his talents.

'Inspector?' The innocent tone of the next enquiry echoed Andrews' earlier approach. 'Inspector, wasn't Junor the name of the cousin in the Ashmore case?'

There seemed no real point in denying it, making himself look more of a fool.

'Yes,' he said cautiously. 'I believe it was.'

He excused himself then, and began to move towards his car making the usual proclamations about there being nothing further he could say and they would be kept informed. He left Bill, the image of the old-fashioned 'traditional' policeman, to calmly talk down the rest of the questions and to follow after him.

He had his hand on the car door when a voice behind him made him look back. Philip Andrews.

He must, Mike thought, have been Tynan's contemporary. A grey-haired man, thinning a little on top, with more lines around his eyes than anyone had a right to and a slightly crooked nose, as though it had once been broken and healed badly.

'I've nothing further to say.' Mike felt annoyed at the irritation that showed in his voice. Why should he have let this man's questions rattle him so much?

'But that *was* Cassie Junor,' Andrews pressed, his tone making it half-statement, half-question.

Mike didn't bother to reply. He got into his car and wrenched the ignition far more abruptly than he needed to, slamming the gears into first. His rear-view mirror showed Andrews and his photographer watching as he drove away. Mike paused along the road, just long enough to allow Bill to climb inside and settle himself in the other seat.

'Well, that didn't go too badly,' Bill commented, his voice and eyes reflecting the amusement he felt at Mike's fit of pique.

'Didn't it?'

Bill looked sideways at him. At moments like this rank took second place to experience. He spoke quietly, 'They were bound to get wind of it, Mike. It's not the kind of thing you can keep quiet for long.'

Mike shrugged irritably and Bill settled back and allowed the silence to grow, letting his boss choose his own pace.

'This Andrews. You know him?'

Bill nodded. 'He's been useful in the past.'

Mike snorted. 'Is that what you call it?' He paused, then let out what was really on his mind. 'Flint's just going to love this. Right prat I'm going to look going in there and telling him, sorry, sir, but one kid isn't enough for them. We'd better start looking for the other one all over again.'

Bill glanced sideways at him, keeping his mouth tight and still but unable to keep the humour from showing in his faded blue eyes.

For a moment, Mike Croft glared at him, then he relaxed. 'OK, OK, so Flint's not the kind that's pleased at anything.' He paused, sobered again, remembered just what was at stake here. 'Can you imagine what her parents must be feeling? The Ashmore girl's, I mean. It will be like reliving the whole thing over again.'

He frowned at the curving road ahead of them, his hands tightening on the steering wheel. He knew what happened to him every time he heard of a child killed in an RTA. Worst of all, if, as had happened with Stevie, the driver had failed to stop. However many times the doctors had told him that Stevie must have died practically the moment he was hit, he still kept asking himself, what if the driver had stopped? What if he'd stopped and been able to help; got help to Stevie just that minute or two sooner. Would it have made a difference? Logic had no place in that kind of thinking.

Would the Ashmores be making the connection? When they found out that Cassie Maltham had been there a second time, would they find her guilty, just to give themselves a reason to cling to? Didn't Mike, every time he saw the report of a hit and run, wonder if that driver was the one that had killed his son?

He made the turn onto the broader, slightly straighter Norwich road and increased his speed a little. Then he turned his attention back to the journalist, Andrews.

'So,' he asked again, 'what about this Andrews?'

Bill smiled slightly. 'Not much to tell, really. He's worked for the *Chronicle* so long they're likely to put him in the archives when he finally pops it. He's essentially honest and very forthright, but he's never seemed to have any hankering for the big time.' He shrugged lightly and slightly lopsidedly. 'A man that's found his niche, I suppose. Maybe that's worth more than most things.'

Mike smiled slyly. If ever there was a man who'd done just that, then it was Bill Enfield. He'd reached sergeant and resisted all attempts to shift him. Liked the personal touch, did Bill, and had a memory that would probably rival the *Chronicle*'s archive.

'And his interest in the Ashmore case? At the time, I mean.'

'Hmm. Same as the rest of us, I suppose. No, it was probably more than most; became as personally involved as Tynan. I remember for years after the case was dropped, the *Chronicle* ran updates and reminders on the anniversary. I know he was in contact with the Ashmores on several occasions, and I seem to remember that it was Andrews that persuaded Mrs Ashmore to make a public appeal about her daughter, both at the time and on the first anniversary.' He paused. 'Poor woman. She looked as though she'd had the life drained out of her. And the father, God, he just stood there, you could hardly get a word out of him. He just held it all in, trying to be strong for his wife I suppose.'

'So, you think Andrews may have kept in touch with the Ashmores for quite some time after?'

Bill nodded. 'Something Tynan never felt he could do. When he knew the case was being officially put on hold – no more evidence you see – he was devastated. Felt he owed it to the Ashmores to tell them himself. I don't imagine it went well. He never talked about it, but he didn't, so far as I know, ever contact them again.'

'How long after was that?' Mike asked.

Bill frowned for a moment, then speculated. 'It must have been a good three years. John Tynan struggled to keep it active for as long as he could, but we were as under-resourced then as we are now. We simply didn't have the manpower available.'

They both fell silent after that, Bill remembering that other time, the other child; Mike letting his thoughts roam the breadth of information covered that day. So, if Andrews had kept in touch with the Ashmores, it might have been only a phone call's worth of time to find out about Cassie Junor, now Cassie Maltham. But why would he have contacted the Ashmores about this? Some strange kind of honour, perhaps, that made him want to be the one to tell them, rather than let them hear it on the news or read the bald headlines in one of the national papers?

Or had he known before of Cassie's marriage and, today, simply hear her name and make the connection?

Cassandra – Cassie – was not so common a name after all.

Perhaps, Mike thought irritably, he had known nothing for certain until Mike had, through his manner and the wayward answers to his questions, given him what he needed.

He frowned angrily, then sighed, allowing some of the tension to ease from where it was lodged around his spine. They were entering the outskirts of Norwich now, the road widening and the suburban landscape taking over. He pulled into the outer yard of divisional HQ, called on the radio for the inner gates to be opened, and braced himself for the coming interview with Flint.

Well, whatever the answers, the thing was done now and that additional factor had to be taken into account.

Was Cassie Maltham guilty? If so, guilty of what?

70

Chapter Eight

Croft made his way through the front office of divisional headquarters.

'Evening, sir.'

He acknowledged the duty sergeant, led Bill Enfield through the barrier and into the station office. Tynan had left them to return home. Croft was about to send Bill the same way, a break before the informal meeting the three had agreed on later to review, among other things, the circumstances of the Ashmore case. They had formed a tacit agreement that their private review should not yet, at least, become part of their official investigation and that Tynan's involvement should be officially ignored as far as possible. Flint, Croft's superior, was going to be far from pleased.

He liked things neat and tidy, did Flint.

Croft deposited Bill in the station office. Bill rarely came to divisional, but he was well known to many of the officers there. He had cleared a desk of its scatter of papers and tea mugs, seated himself and was deep in conversation with the communications officer before Croft had even left the room.

Mike smiled wryly, and steeled himself for his first encounter of the day with Superintendent Flint.

*

Flint was, it appeared, more irascible than usual. He barely seemed to listen to Croft's account of the day's activities, barely give his subordinate time to finish before pushing a sheaf of papers across the desk to him.

'What's this?'

'Usual lists of crank callers, "witnesses" who were nowhere near at the time and, of course, enquiries from our local determined-to-report-the-truth hacks, who inform me that you've re-opened the Ashmore case.'

'It was never actually closed, sir,' Mike pointed out, as Flint paused for breath.

'It was twenty years ago.'

'And we can't discount the possibility that the two might be connected. If I don't consider that angle then you can bet your life someone else will.'

'The press will have a field day.'

'The press already are. Excuse me, sir, but the press have already picked up on it, and on the fact that Cassie Junor, as she was then, has been staying in the village.' He paused, took a deep breath. 'You'll see tomorrow's editions soon enough, no doubt, plastered with pictures of Mrs Maltham and the grieving mother, arm in arm.' He broke off, annoyed at the bitterness in his voice, aware that Flint had noted it.

Flint was frowning. 'The Maltham woman. Do you plan to charge her?'

'With what?'

'Mike, I'm not entirely insensitive. I do know what kind of emotions, understandable emotions, a

72

case like this generates, but we have to tread carefully. The public wants quick results on something like this. Come to that, we all do.' He paused again. 'You really have grounds for seeing a connection?'

Mike relaxed a little. 'To be frank, I don't know. Cassie Maltham has witnesses to the fact that she was elsewhere when the child disappeared. She could have an accomplice, of course, could have planned it . . .'

'But you don't believe that?'

'If she did, she's the coolest most callous bastard I've ever come across.' He spoke quietly, remembering the events in the village hall.

Flint nodded thoughtfully. Then sighed. 'I don't like the way you're handling this, Mike. I want the connection played down.' He looked meaningfully at Mike. 'Talk to Tynan if you feel you have to, we don't want him alienated.'

'No, sir.' Mike didn't try to keep the cynicism out of his voice. 'He might decide he was better served by speaking to someone else. The press, perhaps.'

Flint looked sharply at him. 'Quite,' he said coldly.

He nodded dismissal, made a show of studying the papers on his desk. Mike rose to go. Flint's voice reached him as he lay a hand on the door. 'Play it by the book, Mike. We don't try to be over clever in a case like this, do we?'

Bill was waiting for him in the station office. Tea, too hot and too sweet, just the way Mike liked it, arrived on cue. He found a chair under the scatter of the day's debris, sank down and closed his eyes. If you were going to be official about it, he had his own office, should be there drinking his tea, not here, showing his annoyance and exhaustion to the 'lower ranks'. Flint would not approve, he smiled wryly, knowing that was why he did it.

'Any news, sir?'

He glanced around, and saw one of the new relief just coming on.

He shook his head. 'Nothing yet.' He sighed. 'Early days,' he said with a weary half smile. Stock answer.

The young PC smiled, recognizing it as such. Then said, 'I've never been around something like this before, sir, it makes you feel kind of . . .' He trailed off. 'Got a sister lives out that way, she's got kids.' He looked anxiously at Mike. He nodded sympathetically, not certain what to say. Heard Bill Enfield's voice rumble beside him.

'Tell her what we've told all the parents. Keep a close eye on her kids until this is sorted.'

Simple enough words, but the young man smiled as though they were divine in origin. 'Thank you, sir.'

Croft waited for him to go, then laughed briefly, felt Bill's hand on his shoulder.

'Home,' Bill said. 'Grab something to eat, then I'll meet you across at Tynan's. You know the way?'

'More or less.' Croft swallowed the rest of his rapidly cooling tea, pushed himself to his feet and walked with Bill out to their waiting cars. It had seemed to him like a long day. How must it have felt to Sara Jane's parents?

Mike was the last to arrive at Tynan's. He had not bothered to go 'home' – it seemed hardly worth the trip back to the empty flat. Instead, he'd driven out to the coast, to one of the tourist pubs selling food and basked in the anonymity of the place for a short time. The food had been reasonable, the bar had double doors that opened onto a sea-front terrace, close enough to the water for him to be splashed with spray from an incoming tide.

Carefully and deliberately, he had tried to put work out of his mind, succeeded for all of ten minutes, then given in and allowed his mind to wander from random detail to random detail, trying to see something he'd been too involved to perceive before.

There was a television above the bar. Mike was relieved that he'd arrived in the evening gap between news programmes. He was too far away to hear the sound and left for Tynan's long before the news could begin.

Tynan's cottage suited him, Mike decided. The door seemed to have sunk as though settling itself more firmly into the earth and the new distance had been made up by two steps, somewhat lopsided and cracked. Mike ducked instinctively as he was welcomed inside, was absurdly relieved to find himself in a hallway of more normal proportions.

It had been Bill who had let him in. Through the

open door at the end of the hall he could see Tynan, busy with teapot and mugs. He called out to Mike to make himself at home, Bill led him through a door to the left of the hallway and into the sitting room.

Mike had the sudden impression of a room frozen in time, furnished with chairs, rugs, ornaments that had the look of long residence and were kept as much for sentiment as utility.

He sat down, discovered belatedly that the chair was equipped with rockers and settled more uncertainly into its depths. Tynan appeared with the tea.

'Now,' he said, 'to business.'

Mike watched while he rummaged in the rather cavernous interior of a tall cupboard set against the fireplace wall. It loomed far too big for the small room and it crossed Mike's mind to wonder how on earth they had got it inside.

Then he looked with more interest as Tynan emerged laden down with what appeared to be files and cuttings' books.

'What on earth!'

Tynan grinned at him. 'Everything I've got on the Ashmore case. Others too with a similar MO. All unsolved.'

Mike looked dubious. 'John, I don't mean to put you off, but we've enough with the cases we're working on.'

Tynan deposited the load on the floor, waved Mike's objections aside. 'I know that. No, I'll sort out the stuff that might be relevant.' He shook his head. 'But truly,

Mike. You've no idea just how many kids have gone missing, just from this area alone. It makes you think.'

Mike said nothing. He'd served his probationary year and the two following in London. His ground had covered the King's Cross area. You learnt to pick them out a mile off, the newcomers, there on the off-chance that there was something better. No. He wasn't surprised. He doubted really that Tynan was either.

'But this is different,' he said. 'So far as we know, neither Suzie Ashmore nor Sara Jane Cassidy had either reason or opportunity to up and leave.'

'Agreed.' Tynan shrugged self-deprecatingly. 'You know how it is, though. You hear of one case. It leads on to others—'

'And before you know it you're convinced of a conspiracy to steal the world's children,' Bill put in, his tone more caustic than was usual for him. He apologized at once. 'I'm sorry, John. I guess it's just getting to me.'

Tynan nodded, began to sort through his files. 'Pour the tea will you. Now, let's see.'

Mike watched as he rummaged, casting this file aside, keeping that. Finally he shifted the tea tray over, then deposited a somewhat shrunken but still substantial pile of documents on the table.

'Cuttings, mostly,' he said, 'and reports I wrote for my own records at the time.' He shrugged almost apologetically. 'It's my way of getting things in perspective, I suppose.'

He took his tea, sat back and waited as the other two leafed through the papers.

Mike reached out for another cuttings' book. Seemed every paper of the time had run continual reports for the best part of a month and Tynan had collected just about every one. Mike glanced at him. He knew from experience how it was. Sometimes, a case just got to you, became more important than anything else even when it was obvious it was getting nowhere. Tynan met his gaze steadily.

'Oh, I admit that it was something close to obsession,' he said, smiling slightly. 'But it was the damnedest thing. Weeks, we worked on it and every time we thought we'd got a lead it faded out like so much sea mist.' He shook his head.

Mike sympathized, silently. It was the kind of case that could make or break a career, though, somehow, he doubted that was what Tynan had in mind. The fact that he had not found Suzie Ashmore's abductor seemed to be something Tynan considered a highly personal failure.

He turned back to the cuttings, frowned, then a smile of disbelief spread across his features. 'Witches and fairies, John. Parallel dimensions? What is this?'

Tynan reached across and looked at the book. 'Ah, yes,' he said. 'Problem was, routine police work got well, too routine for our friends in the tabloids. They decided to spice things up a bit. We'd kept the cordon in place for something like a month, after that, well, the moment it came down a whole plague of them moved in with their mediums and their spiritualist hoojas.' He snorted contemptuously. 'Utter claptrap of course, trading on the fact that Tan's hill, you know, that rise overlooking the path, had something of a local reputation.'

'Such as?'

'Some folk nonsense about fairy hills and the like.'

'Oh,' Mike said, losing interest. He had little patience with such things. As it was, the world was too full of ordinary people doing abominable things to other ordinary people for him to want to add some supernatural pantheon to his troubles.

'Get all sorts,' Bill said thoughtfully. Then he added, 'Whether it's true or not doesn't matter. The fact that these things detract from what's important in the investigation is.'

John Tynan nodded. 'Your saying that reminds me of something.'

'Oh?'

'It's the effect all this had on young Cassie. See, she had no memory of the time her cousin actually disappeared, she needed something, anything, I suppose, to help her make sense of it. I had her mother phoning me, mad as hell she was, saying that I had no right to allow the press to publish, now, what did she call them, Demonic Notions, I believe it was. Seems the girl was half-way to believing them.' He shook his head. 'We advised some sort of counselling, you know, disturbed her for a long time. Not that the mother helped.'

'And now. Do you think she was involved?'

Tynan looked straight at Mike. 'No,' he said. 'No, I don't. But, I wouldn't put the dampers on there being some connection, someone who knows she came back.'

'For what motive?'

'Who knows! People don't always have motives they can explain to others, or that make any sense outside their own heads.'

Bill was frowning. 'For someone to know,' he said, 'they'd have to be local.'

'Or someone the Malthams know back home,' said Mike.

'Possible, but they would have to be from Cassie Junor's childhood, not Cassie Maltham's life, for that to make any real sense. Anyway, I'd bet on the local connection. Strangers stick out a mile.'

'The husband, what does he do?'

'Teaches. Combined sciences, as it is now, one of the big comprehensives.'

'Poor bastard!'

Mike laughed.

'And the other two?' Tynan continued.

'Both work for the same company. He's a sales rep,' Bill told him he'd learnt quite a lot in his informal chat with the Thomases and Fergus Maltham earlier.

'Figures.'

'Sells lab equipment and the like. Seems that's how he and Fergus met. His wife's a P.A. for one of the big wigs.'

'Cassie's studying, I believe,' Tynan said.

'Mmm, yes, seems her early education was interrupted by illness, didn't get too far. She's bright enough, so her husband's persuaded her to get back to it.'

Bill fell silent then, frowned down at the stack of papers he was cradling. Mike glanced back at his own mass of cuttings. It was getting late. They were all tired. Time to go maybe. He hesitated. The thought of returning to the empty flat was not an appealing one. Idly, he turned the pages, came to rest at an image of Suzie Ashmore, smiling out of a faded press photo.

'Do you have kids, Mike?' Tynan asked him.

Mike hesitated before replying. 'I did. A son, Stevie. He was killed in a car crash two years ago.'

Tynan held his gaze for a moment, then looked away. 'I'm so sorry,' he said. 'My wife passed on not quite two years ago.' The statement was made like a peace offering. 'It's not the same, I know, I mean, it's not the same as losing a child.'

Mike made no comment. Death hurt, no matter who you lost. What else was there to say. Mike's wife had 'passed on' too, though not in the way Tynan meant. Passed on to another life, another man. He couldn't blame her. Steven's death had shown them both just how little there had been still holding them together. He sighed, rose to go.

'Tomorrow will be a long day,' he said. A lot of long days, probably. Bill rose also, looking slightly awkward, slightly guilty in the knowledge that he was going home to his wife, long-suffering companion of an equally long marriage. He blessed her, silently.

JANE ADAMS

'John,' Mike said, 'I can't offer you any official place in this, you know that, but unofficially . . .'

Tynan smiled. 'Thanks,' he said. Unofficial capacity, standing on the sidelines, careful not to get in the way of the 'real' policemen! Well, it was the best he could hope for under the circumstances. It beat the hell out of racing the kettle. And maybe, just maybe, he could find out at last what had happened to little Suzie Ashmore. Tynan was prepared to accept any position, however peripheral, for a chance of doing that.

82

Chapter Nine

There was a woman in a blue dress. The skirt, reaching to mid-calf, was full and soft, swirling about her legs in the light wind. Cassie ran swiftly, afraid that as she turned from the path to climb the hill, the woman, lost from view for that vital few minutes, would be gone when she reached the summit. Her breath came in sharp gasps. She was aware of the summer heat, the air heavy as though predicting a storm, and, it seemed, however deeply she tried to breath, the air was too thick, too heavy to be drawn into the terrible rigidity of her lungs.

Cassie gasped for breath, fighting against airways that seemed suddenly to be locked solid. Impassable.

The red haze that already floated in front of her was darkening with every step she tried to take. No longer running, by now, almost at the upper curve of the hill, she crawled like a baby on hands and knees.

'Please . . .' She didn't know any more whom she asked, only that three times already her dream had taken her this far and no further. 'Please . . . I have to see her!'

She struggled on. The haze deepening, vision fading, hands clawing at the cool grass, the baked earth. She tried to dig her fingers deeper, her air-starved body fighting for purchase . . . slowly, then more rapidly, she felt herself sliding back, then falling, falling . . . surely she hadn't climbed that far . . . blackness. Breath hardly entering her lungs before that inner constriction forced it back out. Fingers clawed now at empty air. Black air. Living night so dense she could stroke the thick fur of it.

Maybe that was why she couldn't breathe. The air was too thick. Like trying to breath under water . . .

Oh, God! But did it have to hurt so much?

And the woman was gone. Cassie knew that. She wept for her, or tried to. To cry, you have to be able to breathe and the thick blackness pressed on her lungs, drowning her, pulling her down into its killing softness . . .

'Cassie!'

Fergus shook her again, the small choking sound she made frightening him.

'Cassie! Cassie!' He had to wake her.

This time she opened her eyes, looked at him, uncomprehending, then the choking became whimpering, animal like, helpless, and he held her tight. She clawed at him as though she could never get close enough to the safety he promised.

Slowly, she began to relax. Fergus lay down with her, stroking her back, soothing her with half words softly whispered, his face buried in her damp hair. Finally, he asked, 'The dream again?' Felt her nod slightly, her head resting against his shoulder.

'I got further this time.' He had to listen hard to

make out the words, bend his head lower.

'I got close to the top. I knew, if I could just make it that bit further, I'd know . . . something. I'd see her face, then I'd know . . .' She trailed off, began to cry. This time she could breathe, could grieve. Fergus held her closer. Her body slicked with sweat, growing cold now. He reached, pulled the quilt more closely around her.

'Know what, Cassie?' It seemed to Fergus that she should put this into words.

She sighed, shook her head, pulled away from him. 'I don't know,' she said.

Fergus waited, hurt that she should lie to him, trying to understand.

'About Suzie?' he prompted. 'Was it about Suzie?'

Cassie rolled over onto her back, staring hard at the ceiling. Fergus could see her eyes moving idly, as though tracing the cracks in the ageing plasterboard. He tried again.

'Talk to me, Cassie. Don't shut me out.'

She turned her head back to face him, eyes hurt, the dark shadows beneath showing just how little real sleep she'd had in the three days since Sara Jane had disappeared.

'There's nothing to say,' she told him. 'Nothing that makes the kind of sense you need me to make.'

Fergus moved, shifting his weight so that he leaned over her as though preparing for love. 'I don't need anything. I don't expect anything. Cassie, whatever helps you is what I want. If you tell me about the dream, do you think I'm going to judge you? Tell you you're stupid, cracked, or whatever else choice of phrase your mother used. I love you. I want to help . . . and that . . . that's all I know.'

She returned his gaze steadily, the hurt still written clearly in her eyes. Then she sighed softly, shook her head. He could feel the effort it took to shape her words.

'I just knew. Just knew. That if I reached the top, I'd find Suzie. I'd know what happened to her.'

'The woman. She'd be able to tell you?'

'I don't know. Truly, Fergus. I just don't know.'

She turned away from him again and, sighing, he resumed his earlier position, lying beside her propped on one arm, stroking the length of her body, enjoying her softness.

He frowned suddenly. 'The woman in blue. Do you know her?'

He'd asked this before, and she answered with a degree of irritation.

'You know I don't.'

'Cassie. Think for a moment. Your seeing her, it's got to be tied to Suzie in some way.' He paused, trying to get his thoughts in order. 'Supposing, just for a moment, that you saw her then. The day Suzie disappeared, but you lost the memory of seeing her or maybe you just took no notice at the time. Suppose she had something to do with Suzie being abducted. That you saw something but didn't connect it at the time.'

She shook her head. 'No. Believe me, Fergus, the police asked question after question, it would have come out then.'

'Not if you'd buried it. We do it all the time, Cassie, pigeonhole memories we can't or don't want to deal with. They get buried so deep sometimes they might almost have not happened, then, something triggers them and there they are, so strong and so alien that it takes us time to figure out where they come from. Where they fit.'

He could see her trying to puzzle out what he was saying. A small frown creased between her eyes and her mouth seemed drawn tight in concentration.

At last she spoke. 'So, if you're right, what would have triggered it? I mean, I know Sara Jane and all that's happened, but I mean, what exactly?'

It was a long shot, but Fergus figured it might be worth it. 'Maybe you saw her again. While we've been here. Maybe you recognized her, subconsciously, and your mind has been trying to fit the pieces together.'

She turned towards him again. The same half-frown creasing her forehead, but her lips parted now. Questioning. 'But she'd be older. Twenty years older. Would I even recognize her?'

Fergus shrugged.

'I don't know,' he said. 'But I think it's possible. And, if it is possible, I think we should tell the police.'

Her laughter was explosive – and contemptuous. 'What, tell them I've been having nightmares and suggest they look for some woman I've dreamed about?'

She broke off, laughter silenced by the seriousness of Fergus's expression.

'You think they'd even listen to me?' she asked, incredulous.

JANE ADAMS

He sighed. 'Right now, Cassie, I think Mike Croft
will listen to anything and, telling him, telling someone,
getting this thing out into the real world might, if it
does nothing else, help get rid of the nightmares.'

She looked dubious.

'OK,' he said, 'I'll talk to him for you, see if he's
interested or if he thinks I'm crazy too.' He smiled at
her. She scowled, then changed her mind and returned
the smile.

'All right, we'll talk to him. I don't suppose it can
do any harm.' She didn't sound convinced but at least
his giving some sort of rationale to her dream had
eased some of the pain from her eyes. Fergus glanced
towards the window. Light was beginning to filter
through the thin fabric of the curtains.

'It's still early,' he said, his voice coaxing, his hand
moving gently onto her breasts. He saw her eyes widen
slightly, pulled her closer, arms circling her, breasts
pressed against him, hands stroking, one, twining itself
in her curls as she lifted her face to be kissed, the other
tracing the curve of her waist, moving down. He rolled
her over, watching her face as he slid into her. Cassie's
arms reached up, pulling his head down, her mouth
soft beneath his own.

At moments like this Fergus could convince himself
that there was nothing that couldn't be healed. No
pain that couldn't find ease. He laughed at himself.

Pure arrogance, Fergus Maltham, he told himself.
Pure, blessed, wonderful arrogance.

*

88

Mike Croft rubbed his eyes wearily and looked once more at Fergus Maltham. As if he hadn't got enough to cope with. The fourth day and they knew no more than they had that first afternoon.

House-to-house enquiries had continued spreading out over a gradually widening area and police road blocks had been set up, questioning drivers as they came in and out of the area. The one vague lead they'd had, the report of a female itinerant new to the area and seen close to the Greenway shortly before Sara Jane vanished, had drawn a blank. The woman seemed to have disappeared as efficiently as Sara had done. There was a lot of local feeling that if Croft got himself organized enough to find this old woman then he'd find Sara Jane as well. And the rumours that had been flying . . . it was like reading Tynan's cuttings' books all over again. Everything from white slavery to Satanic practices and the whole gamut in between. The press, naturally, were having a field day with the possible connection between this and the Ashmore case. Fortunately, Croft thought, they were still at the 'our children are safe nowhere we must support police efforts' stage. Croft could just visualize the verbal lynching he'd receive if he didn't come up with answers soon.

Now there was this. Mrs Maltham complaining of nightmares. God! He had half the village and a good few of his own people complaining of the same thing. Anxiety seeps like water into the sleep state. He didn't need to be any kind of expert to know that.

He listened though, listened also to Fergus

Maltham's thoughts on the subject. He came to a swift decision – truth was, he'd no time for anything but the swift kind – and organized for the Malthams to talk to a police artist back at Divisional HQ.

'We can drive ourselves,' Fergus said. 'You're over-stretched as it is.'

Croft nodded, amused. The state of play being what it was, he could well sympathize with Fergus not wanting to look arrested and in custody.

'Your friends, the Thomases. They're expected back here at the weekend?'

Fergus nodded. 'That's right. Simon's driving down Friday night straight from work.'

'Right, though I don't imagine we'll be needing them again.' He excused himself as he was handed the last batch of phone messages. He sighed. 'Well, thank you, Mr Maltham, Mrs Maltham. I'll be interested to see what the artist comes up with.'

They rose to go, looking awkward and somehow out of place. Croft dumped the messages on the table, rubbed his eyes again and flexed his shoulders, trying to ease some of the tension which seemed to have settled in a hard lump centre-back.

He'd changed his opinion of Cassie Maltham, decided that, if she was involved, it was as pawn rather than protagonist. The Malthams had volunteered to stay on another week, moving into a caravan on the clifftop, the cottage being booked for the following seven days. The Thomases had gone back to work, annual leave having ended, and new holiday-makers had come to take possession of the vacated cottage; he'd seen them. Young couple with children who, doing their best to enjoy the one week of the year when they could afford to 'get away from it all', had landed, abruptly, in the midst of someone else's crisis.

Mostly, he noted, they'd gone out early in the mornings, come back late, as though embarrassed to be seen enjoying themselves in such close proximity to tragedy.

Mike sighed.

Life must go on, as they say. Even Mr Cassidy had escaped this morning, gone to put in a few hours at Top Farm, leaving Mrs Cassidy to work her way through her own notion of normality. Mike felt so helpless in the face of their grief. He was aware too, that everyone else involved in this, from his own officers to the most hardbitten of the journalists who plagued his every move, were affected, deeply, by the disappearance of Sara Jane Cassidy.

The thought of the child – if she was by some miracle still alive – maybe terrified and hurt, tore into him. If it had been Stevie . . .

Realistically, he was well on the way to admitting that Sara was likely to be every bit as dead as Stevie was. His son had died quickly. The doctors all agreed that he'd probably not even known what hit him. Mike clung to that belief like a talisman, but what of Sara? The thought that she might have died in pain, scared, crying for comfort . . . he pushed the thoughts from his mind. How could any of them even function with

91

images like that flooding their consciousness?

Resolutely, he turned back to the messages received. Most were crank calls or from those who thought they'd seen the child. False or not, every one would have to be checked. He could now well understand Tynan's obsession with the Ashmore case, his feeling that he could never let go, never give up. There were moments when he felt himself drowning, not just in the emotional floodwaters of the case but also in the sheer weight of trivia that might, but probably wouldn't, lead to some solid conclusion.

He'd set John Tynan the task of reviewing the Ashmore case once again. Tynan had the freedom to go and talk to people unofficially that Mike's position did not give him.

From Tynan too, Mike had learnt more about the child, Cassie. Learnt to pity her. That worried him. He'd asked himself again if Cassie could have been directly involved either time. Tynan had spoken of treatment for depression. His layman's mind had immediately taken leaps it shouldn't have. He'd reminded himself abruptly that his ex-wife had also had treatment for severe depression following the birth of their son. It was hardly a reason for assuming Cassie Maltham to be some kind of psychopath, magically abducting children at twenty-year intervals.

No, there were going to be no clear answers to this one. That, if nothing else, was certain.

It was late when Mike arrived at Tynan's cottage. The day had ended with a difficult interview with

Superintendent Flint and an equally difficult update for the press. Flint had not been impressed by Mike's efforts so far (predictable), had, however, made no useful suggestions for revising Mike's methodology (also predictable) and made his usual statements about the public expecting swift results. Mike was, not for the first time, left wondering about the truth in the rumour that they rewarded ineptness by promotion, thus getting the thinking-abouts out of the way of the doers.

Tynan greeted him at the door. He looked as tired as Mike felt. In the background, the kettle had begun to whistle. Tynan almost fled to the kitchen to rescue them both from the piercing scream about to follow. Mike followed him.

'Bill might be along later. I've told him to spend some time with Rose, he's scarcely been home in the last three days.'

Tynan nodded. 'Anything new?'

Mike leaned against the door jamb, peering at the tiny, neatly set out kitchen. Why couldn't he keep his flat this tidy? 'Nothing very significant. Thought you might like to see this though.'

He reached into an inner pocket, removed a copy of the drawing the police artist had produced. The photocopy had, as usual, reduced the shading to mere echoes of the original intent, lost the finer details, but it was close enough.

'Familiar?' he asked.

Tynan shook his head. 'Can't say that she is. Who is she?'

Mike sighed. It had been too much to hope that

Tynan would recognize the woman as someone involved with Suzie Ashmore.

'Truth is, it could be anyone.'

'So, if she could be anyone, why have you wasted the expensive and limited time of one of the divisional's portraitists?' He was smiling. Encouraging. Mike had been asked an almost identical question by his superior a few hours earlier, though the encouraging smile had been significant by its absence.

Tynan picked up the tea tray. The pot, Mike noted, was decorated with a bright green cosy topped off with a bunch of what looked like red cherries. Tynan saw him looking, laughed, half fondness, half embarrassment.

'Grace used to knit them for church fêtes, that sort of thing. Seems we always ended up with the ones no one wanted to buy.' Again that self-deprecating smile Mike was beginning to know so well. 'Old habits and all that.' He ushered Mike through to the sitting room.

Tynan listened attentively while Mike explained about the 'Portrait of an unknown woman', made no comment as Mike related Fergus's interpretation, then looked again at the face.

The woman looked to be in her late-forties, round-faced, hair that looked as though it should have been straight, but curled artificially.

'Doesn't look permed,' Tynan commented.

Mike smiled. 'No,' he said. 'I'll tell you what it makes me think of – when my sister was little, she had hair straight as pumpwater, always wanted curls, our mother said she was too young to use tongs or whatever else, so our great aunt taught her how to tie it in rags. She bound it damp and twisted it somehow.' He grinned. 'I forget the technical details, but it came out looking like that, sort of old-fashioned and softly frizzy.'

Tynan nodded. 'I didn't think anyone did that any more, but yet, I know what you mean.'

He continued to gaze into the woman's face. 'Blue eyes?'

'So Cassie Maltham seems to think, and what she described as fading blonde hair.'

The hair was soft, slightly limp, fluffed out around the face but with no appearance of solidity. It gave a childish look to the face, which itself had a blankness, an emptiness, though, of course, that could be simply the artist's interpretation. It was somehow not a modern face, it would have looked more at home in some stiffly posed daguerreotype, where you knew the sitter had been braced at neck and waist against any sudden urge to move.

Tynan shook his head again. 'No, Mike, I don't know her, but I'll take this with me. It's just possible he might jog a memory somewhere.'

Mike leaned back in the chair, bone weary, he could have slept where he was. He'd toyed with the idea of handing the picture over to the pressmen at the evening's update but Flint wouldn't hear of it. He'd not pressed the point, instead he'd held the idea in reserve for the time, inevitably to be reached very soon, when Flint would be glad of anything he could hand out that looked as if progress was being made. He closed his eyes, dimly heard John suggesting that there was a spare bed upstairs only in need of sheets and, equally dimly, his own voice accepting. Anything was better than the drive back to his empty flat. Wearily, he pushed himself to his feet, picked up the tray and headed slowly for the kitchen.

'I'll see to the pots,' he said. 'Earn my keep.'

Tynan laughed and headed off to find the sheets.

Chapter Ten

The dream came to her again, but this time it was different. Cassie no longer tried to run, allowed herself instead, to drift, as though carried by some invisible, intangible force towards Tan's hill.

The woman waited for her, blue dress swirling around her, arms outstretched as though welcoming. Cassie turned from the Greenway and began to climb the hill. This time, she didn't fight to reach the top. She seemed able, by sheer force of will, to rise easily and effortlessly up the slope. In her head, she could hear a voice calling to her.

'Cassie! Caa-ssie!'

For an instant Cassie tried to hurry, felt the resistance return and forced herself to relax, to give in to the strange current drifting her slowly towards her destination.

She could see the woman clearly now, though she stood with her back to Cassie, face turned away. Cassie approached, reached out towards her. 'I'm here.'

The woman turned, outstretched arms ready to embrace, fingers extended as though she couldn't move from that spot, couldn't quite reach out far enough to draw Cassie to her.

'Cassie . . .' The voice was soft, whispering inside her head. Cassie reached out again, longing to touch, to make that last effort to contact but her feet seemed to be sliding backwards. Looking down, she saw her body, her legs being extended, stretched, as though something pulled her down from the hill but her will to be there kept her hands reaching, her upper body still and untouched. For a moment, Cassie found herself examining this strange phenomenon. Some part of herself knew she was dreaming, wondered which particular cartoon this ridiculous effect was from. Some other part of her mind railed against the distraction it offered, ordered her to look back at this strange woman, reach out that little bit further, hold tight.

A slight gasp made her turn. She stared, horrified as the woman, mouth open now in some parody of a scream, hands thrown abruptly above her head, was sucked down, swallowed whole and alive into the hill itself.

There were seconds when Cassie could not act, she fell forward as though drawn by the other's momentum. Then, as though someone at the other end of herself, that part where her feet disappeared down the hill, had given a sudden jerk, she felt herself retracting rapidly. Body and legs compressing, squashing back into their original form. Cassie hung on, trying to dig her fingers into the grassy slope, but there was no purchase. The dew-dampened grass came away in her hands. Her nails dug into the earth, only to be torn away again by the urgent pulling on her ankles.

Cassie woke with a sudden jolt as though falling from a great height. She lay still, trying not to waken Fergus, then on a sudden impulse, held her hands in front of her face, inspecting them closely. Somehow, she was not surprised to find still-damp mud caked beneath her fingernails.

Mike had slept well, better perhaps than for weeks previously. He lay still for a time, enjoying the feeling of waking actually rested and the small sounds that told him John Tynan was already up and about. Reluctantly, he hauled himself out of bed and made his way to the tiny bathroom. By the time he had dressed and gone downstairs, remembering from last night's painful experience to duck his head when the stairs changed direction and the ceiling lowered unexpectedly, Tynan had the tea made and breakfast almost cooked.

Mike's stomach protested. He rarely ate breakfast, the smell of cooking that early in the morning was slightly nauseating. He took a few sips of tea, steeled himself for the ordeal, aware of Tynan's amused smile and found, much to his surprise, that after the first mouthful it tasted OK. After the second, he gave in and admitted that he was actually hungry.

Both men ate without really speaking, the silence companionable, both so used to their own company that absence of conversation was normal rather than disturbing.

Finally, Tynan poured them both more tea and asked Mike if he had slept well.

'Thank you. Yes, I did.'

John Tynan nodded thoughtfully. 'Thought I'd follow the coast road today, out towards Eccles.'

'Oh?'

'Mmm, it occurs to me that if Fergus Maltham's right, well, it stands to reason this woman's actually staying in the area. She's not likely to want to get too close, most likely pick one of the bigger tourist places to stay in or maybe one of the b. & b.s. God knows there are enough to choose from. There's a chance someone might recognize the picture.'

Mike nodded, it was reasonable enough. 'As you like,' he said, 'but you may want to hold off. I'll like as not be posting that to the press corps late today or tomorrow.'

'I'll do it none the less, I know I won't cover as much ground but I'm going to aim for a particular market.'

'Oh?' Mike said again. What was it about people round here? He'd thought Bill Enfield was bad enough, delivering, as he did, everything in instalments. Now Tynan was doing the same.

'Local knowledge,' Tynan said. 'There's quite a few businesses round here been in the family for a long time. People who come this way regular like, they tend to use the same hotel, same boarding house year in year out.'

'It's a bit much though, isn't it, John, to expect that this woman's a regular? We don't even know she exists.'

100

Tynan sighed. 'You want to tell me one thing in this case that isn't a bit much? Mike, if you can come up with one theory that isn't held together with sticky tape, one set of events that isn't choked with coincidences, then I want to know about it. First, there's Cassie Maltham being here again. Two, there's the disappearance of a kid from the same place. Three, it happened at almost the same time of day and practically in full view of others.'

'Full view is pushing it a bit, both times round,' Mike objected.

'Yes, well, maybe, I'll give you that one. Four, the kids even look similar – blonde hair, blue eyes, little bit on the plump side.'

'The ages are different.'

'All right, the ages are different. Five, there's no logical way either child could have left the Greenway except by going back the way they'd come or by going the full length and coming out close to the estate in full view of half a dozen windows.'

'People don't notice kids, they come and go all the time.'

'They notice, even if it's after the event, especially if that child isn't there any more. They remember. No, Mike, you can play devil's advocate all you like, but you can't deny the coincidences.'

Mike shook his head. 'I'm not trying. I'm just frustrated by them. Well, if you want to give it a go, hawk the picture round and see if you can come up with someone, memory the size of an elephant who remembers the woman now and twenty years ago. I'm willing to look at anything.' He laughed. 'Though I guess you've noticed that already.'

He pushed his chair back, took his plate and cup over to the sink.

'Leave it, Mike. I'll sort them out later, you'll want to be off.'

Mike nodded. 'Thanks then. I'll catch up with you later.'

Tynan remained at the table, listening to Mike organize his departure and drive off. He took the picture from where he'd folded it inside his jacket, looked long and hard at the image. Yes, he'd thought so last night but not wanted to say anything that might mislead. There *was* something, something familiar about the face. Try as he might though, he couldn't place it.

Mike found himself driving out of the village once more, choosing not to stop off at the incident room but go instead to the place where the Greenway branched away from the main road.

The police cordon was still up, red and white stretched across the gap, a young constable on duty. Mike had been tempted to remove the permanent police presence from the scene. It served little purpose and the officer, left there feeling useless, could be better used elsewhere. But Flint had insisted . . .

He got out of the car, exchanged a few words with the officer and continued up the path.

It was an odd sort of place. Banks and hedges rising high on either side, blocking any view of the adjoining fields. The hedges, properly made, plashed and braided at the base, were impassable for anything larger than a cat. He walked on, reaching that point at which the path divided. The old Greenway led on, straight up the hill. The newer path, made a few centuries before for the convenience of the local farmers, veered off, emerging after a hundred yards or so onto another road and facing the small council estate where Suzie Ashmore had lived.

Mike turned, took the old pathway, following its curve up the side of the hill.

What the hell was *she* doing here!

Mike's first thought was anger that the young policeman he'd just spoken to had made no mention of Cassie Maltham, never mind that he'd taken it upon himself to let her past.

At first he just stared at her, bemused by her actions. It was as though she was looking for something, pacing back and forth in some small, defined area, dropping to the ground, feeling her way as though she searched for some hidden door. He watched as, still kneeling, she raised her fists, hammered at the ground. She seemed to pause, look up and around her, head tilting this way and that as though to define the origin of some sound Mike could not hear.

She's nuts, he thought. All of this has pushed her too far and she's flipped over the edge. She hadn't even noticed him, so preoccupied was she with this mysterious search of hers.

He hesitated, wondering if he should expect violence from her when he tried to intervene, or if she was in some sleepwalking state. Was it really dangerous to wake sleepwalkers? He didn't know.

He was almost upon her now, dropped down slowly to crouch just a few feet from her. She was sobbing quietly, desperately. Mike frowned. 'Cassie? Cassie what are you doing?'

The sobbing continued but she paid him no attention.

'Cassie.' This time he reached out and touched her. She cried out as though he'd caused her pain, leapt away from him, but finally looked his way.

'Cassie. What are you doing here?'

'What?' She was looking around her now as though just awaking from some dream state. He wondered if she even knew where she was.

'Can't you hear her?' Cassie looked around, frowning. 'Can't you? Oh, but she's gone now . . .' Then, angrily, 'Did you make her go? Did you? Did you?'

Mike rose and took an instinctive pace backward. Then stood his ground, kept his voice as normal as he could and asked, 'Did you hear someone, Cassie?'

For a moment she didn't answer him. Her mouth hung slack, hands moved but with no real purpose.

'I heard her.' She sounded hurt, confused and child-like now.

'Heard who, Cassie?'

Her shoulders sagged now, she looked utterly defeated, too tired to move or care any more.

'Oh, God,' she whispered. 'I dreamed it, must have. Thought I heard Suzie.'

She lifted her head now, though the effort was obviously almost too much for her.

Mike held out a hand. 'Come on,' he said, 'I'll take you back to Fergus.'

She nodded, took his arm and, leaning heavily on him, allowed herself to be led down the hill.

'What happened to your shoes?' Mike asked her.

Cassie glanced down. 'Must've forgotten them,' she said.

'Didn't my constable try to stop you?'

She looked confused, passed an aimless hand in front of her eyes. 'I don't remember,' she said. 'Don't even remember how I got here.' She had begun to sob again, softly at first but now, as they made their way back to the road, more loudly, more desperately. 'Oh, God! What's happening to me? What's going on?'

Croft put an arm around her, led her, still crying bitterly, down the rest of the path, past the shocked face of the young constable and got her into his car.

Tynan had taken the coast road, heading towards Mundesley. He wasn't, at the outset of his journey, even certain of where he was going or what story he would give to those he planned to question. Instead, as had always been his habit when still on the force, he had simply acknowledged the problem before leaving home and then switched his mind away from it.

He listened to the radio, tuning in to something soothing in the classical line which he vaguely recognized as Tchaikovsky. His wife had liked such music. She could probably have told him what it was and even a little about it. She would certainly have had some views to put forward about the tempo of the piece, whether or not that – what would you call it? – rallentando drew back the flow too swiftly or the woodwind section should have been allowed to dominate quite so much.

Then, as now, Tynan would have been unable to tell whether or not she was right. He always just assumed somehow that she was, had grown so used to her little tirades against the less than perfect, always delivered with such a considered and, perversely, strident gentleness, that he found himself, even now, filling in the silence with the sound of her voice.

Grace would have liked Mike Croft, though, would have approved of him. Somehow, the thought was very satisfying. Somehow, it also made it even more important that he help this younger man to succeed.

Can someone else make amends for another's guilt, however undeserved? Tynan didn't know. But the guilt was there. Had stayed with him for the best part of twenty years – sometimes submerged by other concerns, sometimes buried so far as to give the impression, for a brief time, of having fled but always ready to return when he least expected it.

If he could only know for certain that Suzie was dead it would be a help. Instead, he couldn't help but see her alive and grown up; married perhaps, with children of her own. Existing.

Tynan shook himself angrily. Did it make it any easier on the mind knowing that Grace was well and truly dead? Did absence of doubt really make such odds?

He smiled wryly to himself. Two years on, and another two years of nursing her before that, and John Tynan still couldn't think of Grace as anything other than the woman he'd married. Older, of course, but still with so much life in her and still telling him that she thought the conductor had made that rallentando too soon.

At night, he still fancied he saw her, seated in front of the dressing-table mirror, brushing her red hair peppered with grey, but still thick and glossy, and chatting to him about her day, asking about his.

He almost never thought of her as the woman he had held in his arms that last day, weighing almost nothing. The bright hair reduced to grey wisps and the laughter gone from her hazel eyes.

The road veered off as he saw the first signs for Keswick. He wasn't sure whether it was worth his while asking there, the village being small and there being little holiday accommodation of the type he looked for. On the other hand, it wouldn't take him all that long.

The coast road really was along the coast at this point, as it was at Bacton, the next place up. At high tide in winter, the waves had been known to hurl themselves at pedestrians walking on the far pavement. Today though, the sun was hot and the sea was calm, lazy even, sparkling in the morning light.

Tynan parked the car, locked it and wandered across to lean on the iron railing above the beachfront. He wrinkled his eyes against the glare coming off both beach and water, trying to stare beyond it and out towards the far horizon.

The beach itself was crowded with people, arms and legs bared in the summer heat.

Tynan laughed softly to himself. People-watching had been one of Grace's habits. One of her passions, he supposed.

Grace liked people. Loved their foibles and their silliness. Adored scenes like this when their most attractive weaknesses were so exposed.

God, but he loved her. He felt the muscles of his face tighten in the familiar effort not to show emotion.

Well, no good thinking like that now, he had a job to do.

Tynan began to walk along the front, his gaze turned now not to the beach but to the gift shops, adorned with their plastic buckets and sickly sticks of sugar rock and the small cafés already, though it was only mid-morning, packed to the gills with families. Small children seeming almost to spill from the open doorways.

He crossed the road, drawing the photocopied picture from his pocket as he did so and dodging through the slow-moving heavily smoking traffic. He'd decided, should anyone ask, to drop the ex from his DI status. After all, he'd not been retired that long.

He eased through the door to the first café, wove his way through the crowded tables, the sand-castle buckets and beach bags, and approached the counter, amazed at how easily the official smile and official lines fell back into place.

'Can I help you, sir?'

'Yes, this woman. I wonder if you've seen her . . .?'

Blank looks, replies in the negative, calls to colleagues to take a look and, finally, the apologetic return of the picture.

Tynan thanked them and went out. He'd try the sea-front cafés then slip back into the side streets where the few boarding houses he remembered were located.

The sun seemed to have gained strength even in the few minutes he had been inside. He considered for a moment returning to his car and leaving his jacket inside, dismissed the idea almost at once and continued up the sea front, feeling distinctly overdressed among the throngs of skimpily dressed, brightly decorated holiday-makers.

Wondering if this was such a good idea after all, Tynan opened the door of the second café and stepped inside.

Mid-afternoon found him at Cromer. Keswick had got him nowhere, Bacton had been as bad and he'd decided to try somewhere larger. The drive had been the most pleasant thing about the entire day, taking him through Mundesley, with its restored mill, and Paston, tiny and pretty and very English, half-timbered houses and idiosyncratic twisted roads.

He'd stopped for a late lunch of fish and chips on the Victorian sea front at Cromer, feeling hot and tired and painfully aware of his aching feet, then resumed his tour of the local b. & b.s.

There were hundreds of them. Streets full of semi-elegant Victorian villas equipped with names like Sea Breeze and Blue Horizons, stretching back from the sea front and well into the town. Tynan's third street in seemed to his by now well-practised eye, to be a little more expensive. Perhaps it was the sign boards that were a tad bit more discreet, or the almost inevitable net curtains that were somewhat less yellowed or the paintwork on the frontages that had less tendency to peel.

Whatever it was, this street had an air of prosperity that the previous two had lacked.

The pavement was not less hard though and the sun, well into its afternoon heat, was no less searing for a man now feeling his retirement years.

His door-to-door crusade had attracted attention too. He could see that from the faint but agitated twitchings of the clean white nets and the discreet peering of the inhabitants from their upper windows.

There were several that had suddenly found themselves in rapid need of cleaning.

Tynan wondered for a moment if he had become the

object of suspicion and if he would shortly find himself having to explain his questions to one of his former colleagues.

Would that be amusing – or just plain irritating?

If they offered him a good strong cup of tea while he was making his statement, he thought, it might almost be worth it.

He paused for a moment and stared along the length of the street. It was one of those gently curving affairs, full of similar houses that seemed to go on forever.

He decided he'd go to the end and then give up. His long shot suddenly seemed even longer than before. Already, too, he'd been forced to give explanations he'd rather not have given. Twice, women – and almost all of his interviewees today had been women – had asked him straight if this was anything to do with the missing child.

Other times, he'd felt the need to make the connection himself, though in the most tentative of ways. He comforted himself with the thought that Mike planned to release the picture soon anyway.

He plodded up the entrance stairs to the next house.

It was, again, one of these three-storey affairs, with a basement, the small area in front of which was cluttered with large pots of red geraniums and trailing allysum. The wrought-iron stairway had not escaped the floral touch either. Ivy and wisteria clambered up its length on either side, leaving only the handrail clear. The steps looked well scrubbed and the pale blue and white paint on the front door and what seemed to be original sash windows looked fresh and newly cleaned.

There was a discreet, black-lettered no vacancies sign hanging from a rubber sucker in the bay window and a formal, professionally sign-painted arch-shaped plaque above the door which declared its name to be Ocean View.

Tynan couldn't help glancing around to see if there was.

Maybe from the attic windows, but certainly not from here. Just a view of a long, dusty, Victorian street.

The door opened even before he had a chance to ring the bell.

'I don't buy on the doorstep.'

'I'm not selling.'

She looked distinctly affronted. 'Oh? And what are you meant to be doing then?' The woman, bleached-blonde hair taken neatly back from her face in an old-fashioned chignon and rather childish pink lipstick marring a strong but attractive face, glared at him.

'You think I haven't seen you knocking on doors. What is it?' She looked at the ground beside him, clearly expecting to see some sort of bag containing whatever it was he wasn't selling. She looked back at his face, frowning slightly, a suspicious look creasing the sides of her pink mouth.

'I told you, I'm not selling anything.' He paused, anticipating further objections but none came. Tynan carried on. 'I'm making enquiries about a woman we believe might have been staying in the area.' He held out the piece of paper.

She stared, archly. 'Police are you? How come you're on your own then?' She paused to look up and down the street. 'I thought you lot always travelled in pairs.'

Tynan just smiled and said nothing to disillusion her.

She was shaking her head. 'No, no one like that round here. Artist's impression is it, or whatever it is you call them?'

Tynan nodded, but there was no need for more than that, the woman was in full flow by now.

'I suppose it's about that kiddie went missing?' She gave him an interrogative look.

'What makes you think that?'

She shrugged, looked at Tynan sympathetically as though she thought him slightly soft in the head and in need of sympathy. 'Well, stands to reason, doesn't it? Why else would you lot be checking on boarding houses. Not that it'll do you no good.'

She said this last with an air of satisfaction, thrust the picture back in Tynan's direction and leaned back against the door jamb, arms folded in front of her.

Tynan knew he needn't bother asking her to explain; the trick was going to be getting her to stop.

'I mean, stands to reason,' she said again, 'you let kids play in a place like that and something's bound to happen.' She looked at Tynan for confirmation, then carried on. 'Some places are just meant to be left alone. Kept away from. All them stories you hear tell about that place. Well, there's got to be some reason for it, hasn't there?'

113

Tynan murmured something that sounded like agreement.

'I mean, look at them other two.'

Other two? 'You mean the Ashmore girl.'

'Yes. Her. And that other one.'

'Other one?'

Something jabbed at Tynan's memory, but he couldn't quite place it.

'Yes. Years ago that was. I remember my mam telling me about it. Little thing about the same age. Playing on the Greenway, she was, and next anybody knew, she was gone.'

She paused for breath long enough to note Tynan's interested look.

'Charged her father, they did, but they had to let him go, of course. Never found a body. Not that they'd be likely to, not in a place like that. You mark my words. There's something bad about that place. Something evil.'

Walking back to his car, the heat of the sun making his head ache and his sore feet making him very much aware that he had walked more today than he had done in years, Tynan struggled with the memory.

Damn it! He thought he knew the Ashmore case inside out.

Then it came back to him. A conversation with Phil Andrews when the investigation of the Ashmore case had been at its height. Andrews had lived in the area all his life. He didn't remember the first child personally, the event had taken place a year or two before he had been born, but it had been recent enough for him to remember the adults talking about it when he was a little kid. Well enough for him to have pointed it out to Tynan.

He'd reached his car by now. He opened the door and stood beside it, allowing the furnace-like interior to cool a little before getting inside. He could even recall Phil's words now.

'This isn't the first time it's happened, you know,' he had said. The day had been hot, like this one and Tynan had been standing watching them extend the search to the fields on the ridge circling the lighthouse.

'How do you mean?' he'd asked.

'There was another kid, went the same way. Emmie something. Oh, a long time ago. Nigh on thirty years ago. Must be. Went from the same place.

'They said her father killed her, but nothing was ever proved. Then they thought she might have run away.' He'd shrugged and taken a drink from the bottle he was holding and then offered it to Tynan. 'Makes you think though. Places you think are safe and this happens.'

That's why he hadn't remembered. Fifty years ago now and just a throwaway remark made at the end of a hot and exhausting afternoon.

A bit like this one really.

Tynan eased himself into the still over-heated car and slumped back in the seat. He told himself that he was grasping at straws, that it was pure coincidence.

Wouldn't hurt to take another look at his own record though, or to mention it to Mike – not that the poor sod didn't have enough on his plate as it was.

Wearily, he started the car and began to negotiate his way out of the parking space.

Suddenly the twenty or so miles down the coast seemed like a long, long way from home.

Chapter Eleven

Fergus gazed out angrily over the surging waters. They seemed to reflect his mood. Unseasonably grey, the waves hurled themselves against the foot of the cliff, anticipating the impending rainstorm. Mike watched him.

Fergus had coaxed Cassie into bed and Mike had put out a call for one of the local GPs on the police rota. They had just watched his car drive back down the track towards the village, leaving Cassie sleeping. He'd said little, asked Fergus about his wife's medical history, given her a sedative, and left her to sleep. Mike really had better things to do with his time than wait around for the doctor, but some instinct had told him that it would be wise to wait, that he would learn something. He'd been right.

'Schizophrenia,' he repeated, talking to Fergus's back. 'You never thought to mention this before, Mr Maltham?'

'I told you about the depression, that she'd had treatment.' Fergus swung around, angrily. 'My wife's medical history has no bearing on this case. I've told you the same as I told the doctor, she's not even on medication now.'

Mike sighed heavily, scuffed his toes into the ground and said, 'But you must understand, Mr Maltham, knowing that your wife has a history of mental instability . . . I can't ignore the fact, can't rule out the possibility—'

'That she might have gone completely crazy and abducted two children! How, Detective Inspector Croft? How! Not to mention when. No! Hear me out. Cassie's been a danger to no one but herself. We've been winning. These last two years since she was discharged we've really been winning. Trying to build a life for ourselves. She doesn't deserve this. Doesn't deserve the innuendoes. Doesn't deserve you leaping to the conclusion that because she's been ill she's crazy, and therefore capable of anything.'

'I'm not suggesting she is, Mr Maltham. I'm—'

'Only doing your job. God! Spare me the platitudes!'

'I was going to say, Mr Maltham, that I have a duty to look at all possibilities and that, Mr Maltham, you should credit me with a little more intelligence. Ignorant copper I may be, but I know the difference between psychosis and psychopath and I don't need your school-teacher patronage to remind me of the fact. And . . . if you'll let me finish . . . and I don't need reminding of something else either. Your wife takes herself wandering about like that, in the state she was in. How long is it going to be before the press get hold of it, before the village hears about it and thinks of the inevitable?'

He paused for breath, seeing the uncertainty in

Fergus Maltham's eyes and knew he'd found his mark. He went on quickly. 'They're scared, Mr Maltham. Scared enough not to know or care that Cassie's maybe as much a victim in this as those kids. To put it bluntly, sir, all they'll be concerned about is that there's a nutcase running around loose. They're not going to be worried by the niceties of definition. Do I make myself clear, Mr Maltham?'

For a moment the two men glared at each other. Fergus was the one to back down, shaking his head, his shoulders sagging. He gazed upward for a moment to where the gulls wheeled and screamed, pushing a hand distractedly through his hair.

'God! What a mess. What do I do now?'

The question was rhetorical but Mike answered anyway. 'You tell me all you can about Cassie's illness. What pattern it took, the trigger for it, Fergus.' It was the first time Mike had used his first name and the big man looked sharply at him, resentfully.

'Fergus, I know you don't believe she could be involved, don't want to believe it, but there are others looking for a scapegoat who could cite a dozen cases of murderers and abductors hearing voices.' He could see Fergus's anger beginning to rise again.

'It isn't like that with Cassie.'

'Then tell me what it is like. Help me to help her, Fergus.'

Fergus Maltham looked at him, his eyes narrowed suspiciously and Mike resolutely held his gaze, refusing to back off. 'We have to know, you must realize that.'

He hesitated, unwilling to state the obvious once more, but not knowing any other way. 'I have a job to do, Mr Maltham,' he said quietly, shifting their relationship back once more onto formal ground, distancing himself from Fergus's agony and his own hope that Cassie Maltham was the innocent party in all this.

Fergus nodded. He looked suddenly exhausted, his pallor sea-grey, as though he had aged in the last hour, withered somehow, but there was still a hint of sarcasm in his voice when he replied. 'Must let you do your job, mustn't we, Detective Inspector?'

'Problems?' Bill came over and perched his rotund body somewhat precariously on the edge of the desk.

'What else is there?' Mike had just put the phone down and sat, hand still resting on the receiver, as though waiting for inspiration.

Bill was waiting for Mike to speak. When he did not, Bill began. 'Well, while you're thinking about it, I'll fill you in on the day's events, as they say. It'll take all of five minutes and that's if I stretch it out.' He glanced expectantly at Mike who managed something close to a smile and settled back in his chair.

'Go ahead.'

'Right. We've extended house-to-house, as you know. Come up with two reported sightings of that old woman, the itinerant we'd been trying to track down.' He got up, crossed to the large-scale map pinned to the wall. 'They're both in the same location. Here.

120

Some four miles from the village and both sightings within a couple of hours of each other. One's by a woman called Margaret Fesham, lives out at Ancaster. Happens she was driving about here,' he indicated a place on the map. 'She estimates about a hundred yards or so past this crossroads. Says she damn near ran the old girl over when she wandered out of a field and into the road. It's a sharp bend just here, well, you can see. Mrs Fesham didn't spot her until she came round it.' He grinned wryly. 'She's at pains to say that she was only coming slowly down there, but reading between the lines . . .' Mike nodded. Bill continued, 'Second one was about a mile from there and about an hour later. Seems the old tramp was knocking on doors selling non-existent pegs or something. We had a complaint about her but no one made the connection at the time.' He glanced apologetically at Mike. 'That was two days ago, but it gives us a direction.'

Mike snorted, contemptuously. 'Go on.'

Bill hesitated for a moment, then continued, 'Seems funny to me there haven't been more sightings. I mean, you know what the locals are like for strangers. Well, word went out pretty fast we were looking for her and here she is, not four miles away from the main search area and only two sightings. Seems funny to me too she'd not gone further. I mean, four miles in about three days, not exactly fast going is it?'

Mike frowned, then looked at the map with more interest. 'What it probably means is, she's found herself somewhere warm and dry to hole up at night and travels out from there.' Somewhere she could hide a child? Mike stood up, impatient now and studied the map again.

'We've everyone we can spare still searching out-buildings and we've got local help organized in every village in a ten-mile radius.' Bill shook his head. 'You'd never believe what people dump.'

Mike snorted again. He'd suggested that Bill and the other area constabulary men organize their own teams and local volunteers. They knew the area, every copse, every derelict barn. He'd given orders that any item of clothing, anything in fact that looked out of place, be photographed, its location marked, and the item bagged up and sent to divisional. What SOCOs that could be spared, he'd tasked closer to the village. So far they'd turned up nothing but a big blank – an assorted jumble of old shoes and discarded knickers. Nothing identifiable as Sara's. Mike had chosen to see that as encouraging, though he recognized that right now he was willing to see anything that wasn't actually negative as encouraging. Bill was looking thoughtfully at him.

'Word is the Maltham woman's been acting a little strange.'

Mike looked sharply at him. 'Well, I suggest you make sure word stops,' he said.

Bill's eyebrows raised fractionally.

'OK,' Mike said wearily. 'I waited for Doc Fordham to arrive, had a talk with Fergus Maltham after. It seems Cassie Maltham spent a little time in a secure unit being treated for some form of schizophrenia.'

'Oh?' Bill perked up. 'Well, that looks promising.'

Mike glared at him, then sighed. He'd expected better from Bill but the reaction was, he knew, likely to be a common one.

'Schizophrenia, Bill. It's an illness, not a crime.'

'Well, I know that, Mike, but it's still worth looking at.' He paused, sensing there was more, taking on board the implications as Mike had done earlier. 'It's not something you can keep quiet, Mike. From what I hear she was wandering about on the Greenway, got through our cordon somehow.'

Mike nodded. 'And that,' he said, 'I find far more relevant to the case than Cassie Maltham's previous mental state. Just how did she get through?'

The officers stationed at both ends of the pathway had sworn till they were blue that they'd not left their position. Mike was inclined to believe them. It was conceivable that they might be mistaken, or lying, but add to that the presence of assorted pressmen on both roads and locals making their way to work, taking their kids to school, and it seemed unlikely they were wrong.

The Malthams had been pestered repeatedly to make statements and he'd been seen taking Cassie back to the caravan in his car. Several times that day he'd found himself being asked if she'd remembered something that helped with the case, all of the enquiries came from her being seen in his car; none from her being spotted wandering barefoot on Tan's hill. If there was another way onto the Greenway it meant another way of taking a child off the path without her being seen.

'She say how she got there?' Bill asked.

Mike frowned. 'To be truthful, Bill, she wasn't in much of a state to tell me anything.' He saw Bill's half-triumphant look and added hastily, 'Oh, she was rational enough by the time I'd got her back to the car. She knows what's happening to her, it seems to me she's doing everything she can to get a grip on things.' He frowned again. 'Strangest thing was up on the hill, it was as though she was sleepwalking or something, then when I spoke to her, it was as if she'd woken up from some deep sleep and was horrified to find herself there.'

Bill shrugged. 'Could be a put-on.'

'Could be, Bill. I'm not ruling anything out.'

'How come her old man didn't miss her?'

'It seems he'd gone down to the village, left her asleep. She's not been sleeping well and he thought she'd be better catching up. When he got back she was gone, he'd just started out to look for her when we turned up.'

Bill was frowning thoughtfully, concentration wrinkling the already furrowed face into even deeper lines.

'She'd still have needed an accomplice,' he said. 'No way she could have been in two places at the one time.' He laughed abruptly. 'Not even with a split personality!'

124

Mike glowered at him, then allowed a brief smile. 'No. Which means we either assume we're looking for an accomplice or we cross Cassie Maltham off our list.' He went back to his desk, picked up the artist's impression of Cassie's dream woman.

'You releasing that?' Bill asked him.

Mike nodded. 'Flint wants it to go out. Doesn't believe it means anything but it's something to keep the wolves quiet.'

He flexed his shoulders and smiled wryly. 'I think we might just spare them the story of where it came from though,' he said as he left the office. Bill's laughter echoed behind him.

Fergus was cooking, trying to coax the ageing Calor gas stove to give out something like an even heat in two directions at the same time. It seemed you could have either grill or gas burners at even pressure, not both. He tried shuffling the pans around so that he could squeeze the tiny kettle on as well, spent time puzzling over the best arrangement, welcoming the rather meaningless activity and the way it took his mind off his real problems.

Cassie stood in the doorway watching him. It was several minutes before he became aware of her, giving time for her amusement at this over-tall man, squeezed into this over-small kitchen. She laughed aloud and Fergus almost dropped the pan he was holding.

'Cassie.' He smiled broadly at her, put the pan down

125

and went over to hug her, enjoying the warmth of her through the thin silk of her red kimono.

'How are you feeling?' he asked, keeping his voice gentle as though speaking to an invalid.

'Better. Here, let me help with that.'

She pulled away from him, crossed to the stove and started checking the contents of the pans, suddenly impatient.

Fergus watched her for a moment then said, 'I was worried about you.' His words sounded weak, ineffectual, conveying nothing of the turmoil his thoughts found themselves in.

'I'm sorry,' she said.

He waited, but there was no more. She might have been apologizing for a minor accident, a moment of clumsiness. Fergus felt his normally placid self begin to slide away and spoke with more irritation than he normally allowed Cassie to hear in his voice.

'Sorry! That's all you can say? That you're sorry?'

Surprised, she turned to look at him, then went on fiddling with the pans, pretending to be occupied. Fergus could see her hands were shaking, felt a moment of pity, but his own pain was too close to the surface for him to suppress it.

'Well?' He paused, but again she made no answer, just stood still now, hands loose at her sides. 'Do you know how scared I was, Cassie? Can you even think how much you frightened me going off like that. God! I had visions of them finding you at the bottom of the cliff. Anything.' He crossed over to her, placed his hands almost too gently on her shoulders. 'Cassie, if I lost you . . .'

She turned towards him, eyes pleading. 'I don't know what happened, Fergus. I just found myself there. I remember dreaming about the woman again, then, next thing I know I'm on the hill and Mike Croft's standing staring at me like I've gone completely crazy or something. I didn't mean to go. I didn't *know* I was going.'

Fergus looked down at her, felt his anger dissipate as swiftly as it had come. What was the use of it anyway? He began to marshal his thoughts for the questions he knew he had to ask her and held her close, fingers stroking her curls, tugging them straight, releasing them to spring back.

'Oh, Cass. Ignore me, love, it's just the fear talking, you know that.' He felt her nod, then holding her away from himself slightly, plunged straight in. 'He said you heard voices, heard Suzie calling to you.' He so desperately wanted her to deny it. Auditory hallucinations, Dr Lucas had called them, he remembered that, it had been one of the later symptoms of Cassie's illness. She smiled, a little wearily, and shook her head, turning now to rescue their meal from the very real threat of burning.

'It wasn't like that. Not like last time. Fergus, I'm not sick.' She paused, moving the pans onto the counter. 'Hope you like soggy potatoes.'

'Mash them.'

'I'm not getting sick,' she repeated. 'Confused – I

127

don't know what's going on in my head – but it's not like before.'

He frowned. Looked sharply at her, wanting to believe. It was true as far as it went. This wasn't like the psychosis she'd experienced last time. That had been insidious, so slow and so subtle he'd been able to convince himself that there was nothing really wrong until her condition had become serious. Her self-loathing had become so strong he'd not dared to leave her. No, this wasn't like that. But did these things always follow the same pattern? Last time, there had been a kind of religious mania, a ritualization of actions, seeing of signs and omens in the most everyday experiences. Would it happen like that again?

Cassie sighed in exasperation, handed him a fork. 'Sorry this place doesn't run to sophisticated gadgets like potato mashers.' She looked sideways at him, then turned to face him fully, a half smile playing around the corners of her full mouth. 'Now, listen here, Mr Fergus Maltham. Your wife isn't nuts, isn't about to get nuts and isn't about to find mystical significance in the absence of ordinary cutlery. But if you keep her waiting for her dinner much longer, she's likely to get real mad and feed your share to the seagulls. Now, get mashing.'

Fergus laughed in spite of himself and was rewarded by Cassie smiling properly at him. 'We've come too far, love, I'm not about to throw it away. If I thought for one moment I needed help, we'd be in that car and driving back to Doctor Lucas faster than you could even think of it.'

He hesitated for a moment, then said softly, 'But what if you don't know? Cassie, maybe you're not the best person to recognize the signs . . .'

'Then you tell me. You think I'm crazy?'

He hesitated again, then shook his head. 'No, Cassie. I don't know what's going on and I know you've been disturbed by this. I think maybe we should phone Doctor Lucas, get some advice?'

She nodded. It made sense. 'It was more like sleep-walking,' she said. 'More like I was dreaming. When I was a kid I used to do that. My mum used to have to lock the doors and shut all the windows or I'd be gone. Usually I'd wake up in the next street or something.'

'You told me that they said it started when your father walked out, right?'

Cassie nodded. 'Not so uncommon, I'm told. Bit like some kids start wetting the bed when something bad happens.' She took the potatoes from him, began to serve them. 'I figure it must be something like that. Something bad's happened and I'm dreaming about it, the dreams are getting a bit too real and I'm walking, trying to look for a physical solution.'

'It makes a kind of sense,' he admitted and carried the plates to the table. What Cassie was saying did make sense. If only he could be sure. Doubt wrote itself like an insult at the corners of his mouth, drawing them down tightly. Whatever happened, he promised himself, they could beat it. But he remembered the long process Cassie had been through before. The drugs, the therapy, the daily hospital visits to a woman he no longer recognized as his wife. Cassie's own long journey of rediscovery, of remembering who she was, who he was, what they'd had together. He loved her, more than he could find words for, but, remembering all of that, he wondered if he had the strength to help her fight the demons a second time.

It's not going to happen again he told himself. She was just sleepwalking this time.

He carried the tea things to the table, forcing himself to smile at his wife, intent on manufacturing an aura of comforting deceit and knowing that she could see straight through it. She looked away, forcing herself to concentrate on her food though the effort to swallow almost choked her.

'I'll pour the tea,' Fergus said softly.

Chapter Twelve

The news broke early. Another child missing, the village already in turmoil and no hope this time of doing anything unhampered by the pressmen camped in close proximity to the incident room. Mike had again stayed at Tynan's. Bill Enfield called him there and he and Tynan drove straight over. It was just after seven-thirty a.m. The child, Julie Hart, had been reported missing less than an hour before.

'How long has she been gone?'

Bill shrugged. 'Impossible to say. Her mother went to wake her for school and found the bed empty, Julie nowhere to be found.'

Mike frowned. There may be no connection, the child might simply have wandered off somewhere. He gestured towards the incident room. 'The mother's there?'

Bill nodded. 'The Cassidys too.' He grimaced at Mike's sharp look. 'Not a lot I could do about it, sir, feelings running pretty high.'

'Give prizes for understatement around here do they, Sergeant?' He started towards the village hall, ignoring the questions being hurled at him from all directions.

The Cassidys and Mrs Hart were seated at the far end of the hall. Mrs Hart was in tears, the two women doing their best to comfort one another. Mr Cassidy paced like something too long caged, and turned angrily on Mike the moment he saw him.

'How many more do there have to be? Our kids go missing and you sit around on your fat arses doing fuck all about it. Why aren't there more men here? Why haven't you found the bastard that's doing this?'

Mike paid him no attention. The man wasn't about to listen anyway. Instead, he crossed to where the two women sat. 'Mrs Hart?'

'Yes.'

'Mrs Hart, can you tell me what happened? Please, Mr Cassidy, Jim, we're not doing any good just hurling abuse at each other . . . Mrs Hart?'

Cassidy was still shouting, but it was clear he was winding down, as close to tears as either of the two women. These last few days have aged them, Mike thought. The man's eyes were red-rimmed by grief and lack of sleep. Dark-shadowed. Mike pushed a chair towards him and he sat down wearily as though suddenly deprived of power.

'Mrs Hart,' Mike prompted again, but the woman seemed unable to hold together long enough to answer him. It was Janice Cassidy who spoke for her.

'She went to wake Julie up as usual and she wasn't there. She went up and down the street calling for her, came running to us, she hasn't got a phone, you see.'

Mike nodded. 'Had her bed been slept in?'

The mother managed a nod, then burst out, 'She's a good girl, my Julie, a good girl.'

'I'm sure she is, Mrs Hart, I'm sure she is.' He paused for a moment, addressed his next question to Janice Cassidy. 'You've checked that she's not with friends?'

The woman nodded. 'First thing we did was phone round all we could think of.' She hugged the distraught woman closer, finding strength to fight her own tears by dealing with someone else's need.

'Look,' she said. 'Jim and me, we'll take her back to our place. Could you get someone to leave a note for Denny?'

'Denny?'

'Her boy. Helps Ben Fields do the milk round. He'll be back any time now and wonder what the hell's going on.'

'Right,' Mike told her. 'You take her home with you and I'll get the doctor sent out, give her something to calm her down. All right to tell Denny to come to you, is it?'

Janice Cassidy nodded, helped Mrs Hart to her feet and began to lead her away. Mike instructed two of his officers to escort them home and relay the message to Denny. He was about to leave when Bill called him aside.

'You ought to see this.'

He dumped the morning editions on the table. Mike looked. Most carried the image of the dream woman with some variation on the WHO IS THIS MYSTERY WOMAN? theme.

133

'It's this one, Mike.'

Croft looked; cursed loudly. It had to happen, he knew that, but why now?

'Seems they tracked down Cassie's mother, Mrs Junor. Seems she told them every damn thing.'

Mike was reading. It was all there. Cassie's illness, the symptoms, the inferences, the insinuations: all the things Mike and Fergus had so dreaded.

'I want someone up at the caravan – *now*! Tell the Malthams to stay put.'

'Right.'

Resolutely, Mike tensed himself for the questions that would be fired at him the moment he left the hall. He wondered just how long it would be before the entire village had read Mrs Junor's hysterical account of her daughter's sickness, of the voices she heard, the so-called visions. The writer of this particular 'exclusive' had been careful not to make any suggestion that Cassie was violent, a threat to anyone. The account had been sympathetic, a look-what-this-poor-woman-has-had-to-endure angle. The destructive part. The part that made Mike go cold was the juxtaposition on the same page of a brief résumé of famous cases. Murders. Kidnappings. Ritual mutilations. All, of course, carried out by those with some form of mental illness. By those who heard voices, saw visions, had episodes of selective amnesia. The inference was clear and it scared Mike to death.

The phone began to ring. Some intuition told Mike that his superior had just been presented with the same colourful résumé of the 'facts'. He hurried towards the door, yelling back over his shoulder, 'I've already gone.' He left the hall and began to push his way through those crowded outside and towards his car, beckoning Tynan to follow.

'I have to go, Fergus. Look, just indulge me. I don't expect you to understand, just go with me.'

He looked anxiously at her. 'All right, we'll go. But, Cassie, they probably won't even let us through the cordon and unless you can remember how you got through last time . . .'

She gave him an exasperated look. 'It'll be all right, Fergus. Trust me, I have this feeling about it.' She saw him frown again, shook her head and began to pull on her clothes. This time she remembered her shoes.

Reluctantly, Fergus followed suit. It was Cassie's 'feelings' that worried him so much. Still looking for signs?

Before, she had done things, said things because she had a 'feeling' about them. Then, it had been symptomatic of her illness. Now? He just didn't know what to think any more.

'We'll take the car,' he said flatly. He was willing to go with her, but felt like walking nowhere this time of the morning.

They took the back road away from the village. The police car Mike Croft had sent to them arrived via the other road five minutes after they had gone.

*

135

Mike stared at the radio as though he could blame the instrument for the message being transmitted.

'Not there?'

'No, sir, the car's gone, and, sir, we've a group of journalists just arrived up here. What shall I tell them, sir?'

Mike groaned. Didn't these youngsters know anything?

'You tell them sweet FA, Constable. Got that?'

'Er, yes, sir.'

Mike broke contact, did a U-turn in the middle of the road and began heading back the way he'd come. Only one place Cassie Maltham was likely to be headed. Well, at least it seemed she'd taken Fergus with her this time. He glanced at Tynan seated beside him. 'Now what?' The question was rhetorical.

Tynan shrugged. 'You asking me, sonny Jim? This old guy's retired, remember?'

He took the left turn just before the village and saw the Maltham's car parked on the verge. Fergus Maltham was talking to the constable on duty. Bill Enfield was there too, trying to keep control of a TV crew from one of the twenty-four-hour news nets.

Of Cassie there was no sign.

Mike passed the TV crew.

'This is going out live, Inspector. If we could just have a comment?'

Mike curbed his impatience. 'There's really very little I can say at the moment.'

'What about this little girl, Julie Hart? Do you think

her disappearance is connected to that of Sara Jane Cassidy?'

'I think we have to keep an open mind at the moment. It's still possible the child wandered off without telling anyone. Now, please excuse me.'

The anchorwoman followed him as far as the entrance to the Greenway, cameras focused on the small group huddled there. Fergus did his best not to raise his voice though his growing impatience was evident.

'Where's Cassie?' Tynan asked. He'd expected to find her standing beside Fergus, the only position from which they couldn't have seen her as they drove up.

'Cassie?' Fergus turned sharply, the Constable also. 'She was here . . .'

Mike gestured impatiently and led the way through the police cordon just as Bill's radio flared into life. He paused, listening as Mike, Tynan and Fergus charged ahead.

'Mike!' Reluctantly, Croft turned back, surprised at the sudden lack of protocol in Bill's address.

'What is it?' Fergus had paused. Impatiently, Mike gestured for him and Tynan to go ahead.

'The little girl, Julie Hart. She's been found.' He was grinning broadly, relief and amusement beatifying his rounded features.

'Where?'

'Kids!' Bill waved an expansive arm. 'Seems the little madam decided she was going with her brother this morning. Knew her mum would say no if she asked, so she didn't ask, just told the old guy that does the

137

milk round that it was all right. Seems her brother backed her up and the old man just accepted it.' He grinned. 'Bet their poor mam's going to give 'em hell.'

The anchorwoman stood beside them, a fact Bill had seemed to forget. Was he playing to the audience? Mike thought wryly. He nodded satisfaction, turned away once more.

'Going out live, Inspector Croft!' the woman called to him, then turned back to her crew to do the you-heard-it-here-first-folks bit. Mike left the scene in Bill Enfield's more than capable hands and continued up the path towards Tan's hill. There was still a child missing.

Fergus gazed around him, gnawing his upper lip and moustache as he did in moments of real agitation. Where the blazes was she?

Tynan was walking the hill's perimeter, looking down on the Greenway, on the fields beyond, though sense told him there was no way she could have pushed through the plashed blackthorn hedges at the bottom.

'We'll go back down,' he said. 'Walk through to the other end, there's parts of the path I can't see from here.'

Fergus hesitated, then nodded. It was obvious Cassie wasn't here, she must have headed straight along the path and not come up the hill this time, though how she'd got away from them in the first place was more than he could fathom.

They met Mike half-way down the hill.

'They've found Julie Hart,' he told them.

Fergus looked mystified. Stuck in the caravan on the cliff top the morning's events had somehow passed him by. Mike explained, told them where she'd disappeared to.

'Little bugger.' Tynan grinned. 'Well, that gives us one less to worry about.' He frowned, looked about him again. 'Cassie's not up there, Mike, we figured she must have gone on up the path, not come here after all.'

Mike turned with them, began to pick his way once more down the rather slippery side of Tan's hill, the grass, dew-dampened, still not completely dried despite the already warm sun. His mind wandered, coursing around the problems he was faced with. The Ashmore child, long gone but still making her presence felt. Sara Cassidy, seeing her parents again and again over the last few days, their distress deepening every time he told them there was no more news. What could he say to them? And Cassie. What part was she playing in all this?

Mike found his perceptions of her shifted. When he was with her he could identify her as a victim, as an innocent caught in a maelstrom of someone else's making. Away from her, facing the biased, automatic gut reactions of his colleagues he was less sure. Men like Bill, who honestly believed that Cassie's illness was, if not the key to all this, then at least the pointer. But he had doubts, knew how easy it would be to give in and accept the majority ruling.

His mind went back to last night's encounter with

Flint. Mike had admitted he'd not pressed Cassie on how she'd got onto the Greenway unseen. Flint had been demanding explanations. So far as he could see there was only one way; negligence on the part of one or other of the young officers manning the cordons. He'd raged fire and brimstone at them, Mike knew, got both officers to the state where they could no longer be certain they hadn't been looking the other way at the crucial moment.

They were on the path itself now and Mike looked again at the close, tangled hedges. Could they be climbed? He put out a hand, pulled experimentally to see how much give there was, drew back hastily and put bloodied fingers to his mouth.

Not possible, at least not in this section, and not without thick gloves and thorn-proof clothing. Damn it! Cassie hadn't even been wearing shoes!

'Is it like this all the way along?'

Bill nodded. 'You've looked at it often enough, Mike, you know it is.'

Mike grimaced slightly. Bill was right.

Yes, the hedge, well-made and well-kept, would be strong enough to accept the weight of someone Cassie's size without breaking down, and there'd probably be little trace on the hedge of an attempt to half climb, half push through. Somehow though, looking at his sore, still bleeding hand, he doubted the person that tried it would have been left unscathed. And from what he'd seen Cassie had been without a scratch.

No, whatever way he looked at it, it made no sense. No sense at all.

They were approaching the other end of the path now, could see the red and white cordon, the constable manning it and the small group of press and curiosity seekers that had become a feature.

Mike sighed. 'Well, she's not come down here,' he said, glancing at Fergus.

The man was growing more agitated by the minute, looking around him as though he expected Cassie to suddenly emerge from some gap in the hedge, to jump out at them like a child in hiding. He'd been calling at intervals, shouting her name, listening hard for some answer. He tried again now, desperation showing now in his voice.

'Cassie! Caa-ssie!'

Nothing.

Mike cast him a sympathetic look, and was about to suggest they head back the other way when the quiet of the sheltered pathway was ripped apart.

Just for an instant everyone froze, then Mike began to run, the others in close pursuit. The sound was terrifying. An hysterical, almost non-human scream-ing, and it was coming from behind and above them, from Tan's hill.

But there was no one up there. The thought reeled in Mike's head. No one up there. Incomprehension. The screaming grew louder, an animal sound, wounded, unbearable pain . . . then diminishing, becoming a wrenching, heart-rending sobbing.

A child! It had to be. Mike couldn't have said how he knew but the cries were not adult. He was on the hill now, racing up it, slipping. His knee hit the ground and a sharp flash of pain momentarily braced it from hip to ankle. He felt Tynan reach out and grab his arm, saw Fergus just ahead of them, almost threw himself the last few feet onto the summit.

'Oh, my God.'

Cassie Maltham knelt, arms around the weeping child. The screams had exhausted themselves, become deep, painful sobs, stifled because Cassie had turned the child's head, held her close so that her face was buried in the soft fabric of her jacket as though to protect her from seeing whatever it was that terrified her so much.

What it was Cassie protected her from didn't take much discovering. Cassie's eyes met Mike's, she jerked her head sideways and Mike moved across to look down the hillside. A woman. No, not just any woman. The woman in Cassie's dream. Here, for real, and very dead. Very dead, Mike repeated to himself, blackened by the most extensive bruising he had ever seen on anything, twisted limbs, broken bones protruding through bloated skin.

Fergus vomited helplessly. Mike swallowed hard and looked away, gestured for Tynan to take Fergus Maltham down, then walked slowly over to Cassie and the child.

'We should get her away from here,' Cassie said softly. 'I tried but she'd just frozen, I could hardly move her.'

Mike nodded, utterly baffled. He did his best to get his mind in order. Already he could hear voices. Others must have heard the screaming, come rushing from both ends of the pathway. He could hear Tynan's voice, calm and authoritative ordering them back, but Mike knew he couldn't hold out long against the crowd's concern and anger.

He reached out towards the child, touching her hand very, very gently. 'It's Sara, isn't it?'

'Yes.' The reply was more of a strangled sob than a word but at least she was responding to him.

'We're going to take you home now, darling. Home to your mum and dad.'

He stood up, reached and helped Cassie do the same, the child clinging to her as though she'd never let go. They began to move slowly down the hill.

'Where did you find her?'

She hesitated, reluctant, then, 'I don't know.' Cassie's answer rose barely above a whisper.

'Don't know! What the hell do you mean, don't know?' Mike was outraged. It was, he knew, hardly a professional response, but he'd gone beyond those sorts of considerations.

'Mrs Maltham, I just don't think you appreciate the seriousness . . .'

He didn't get to finish, for Sara Jane was yelling at him, had broken free of Cassie's grasp and was pounding at him with small, bony fists.

'Don't you shout at her! Don't you shout at her! She came and found me. In the dark place. You didn't come and get me, nobody did. Leave her alone! Leave her alone!'

She was weeping again, anger burning itself out in

exhaustion. Cassie gathered the child to her once more and led her without Mike's help down the lower slope of the hill and onto the path. Quite a crowd had gathered, Mike noted angrily, but they parted, silently, as Cassie and the child passed through. He could hear voices softly repeating the child's name, found himself suddenly excluded as the crowd drew in again behind the woman and the weeping girl.

'Sir?' It was the young constable from the village end of the cordon. 'Sir, what's going on, sir?'

Mike bit down the urge to tell him that he didn't fucking well know. Instead, he took the best grip on the situation he knew how to, began to give orders for the cordon to be reinstated and strengthened, for SOCO and the path boys to be called in. And he prepared himself for telling Flint they now had a murder enquiry on their hands.

Chapter Thirteen

Mike's head was filled with the day's fragmented images. The morning's events had caught everyone unprepared and found Mike short of senior personnel. Finally, it had seemed best to make use of Tynan and it had been the ex-DI and a young WPC who accompanied the overwhelmed Cassidys and Sara to the hospital for medical checks. Bill had been left to co-ordinate primary activities on site and Mike himself had escorted the Malthams to Divisional at Norwich for interviewing.

It was at that point the day had ceased to be productive, had become instead one long frustrating grind of an anticlimax, consuming time and giving nothing back.

Mike stared hard at the phone receiver he still held in his hand, then, remembering what he was supposed to do with it, replaced it on the cradle and prepared himself for renewed assault on Cassie Maltham's 'memory loss'.

The truth was he didn't know what to make of it, and Bill's call to him from the hospital – where he had joined Tynan – had done nothing whatsoever to alleviate his confusion.

'Well?' Flint's sharp enquiry jolted him back to the present.

'The child claims to remember no more than Mrs Maltham does and she's got no logical reason to lie to us.'

Flint was glaring at him. 'And you can't get the Maltham woman to break her story? She sticking to her Whammy the great magician act?' He paused, slurped at cold coffee and made a disgusted sound as the skin on it attached to his upper lip. Mike stifled the desire to smirk, looked away instead and stared hard at the blotched plasterboard of the office wall.

'And what about our so-called experts? Do they have any . . . insights?'

Croft shook his head. 'Neither our medic nor the shrink we called in can find any evidence of irrationality or psychosis. We can't charge her, sir, we've nothing to charge her *with*. We can't have her sectioned either. The best they can come up with is maybe some neurological problem her own doctors didn't detect, something that causes her to black out, to lose memory of certain times or places.'

'Do they think she could commit murder during one of these so-called blackouts?' Flint asked. He was clutching at straws and they both knew it. Even if Cassie Maltham had murdered the woman there remained the problem of how she had hauled the body up to the top of Tan's hill and got the child there in the few minutes that Croft and the others had been absent. Just how anyone could have done that was beyond Mike's immediate comprehension, to say nothing of where they had hidden the body prior to this, never mind the woman's identity, why had she been so brutally beaten . . . Those questions were just for starters.

'Her husband's called their own solicitor. Called in the Psych that treated her as well, a Doctor Maria Lucas. She's due here at any time.'

Flint made the same disgusted sound again. 'So, and what does she hope to achieve? Anyway,' he went off on a different tack, 'how come they've got their "own" solicitor? What sort of person keeps a brief on tap?'

'I couldn't say.' Mike smiled briefly. 'For all I know he's handled their house sale for them; drawn up their grandma's will. You know how it is, makes people feel better to be able to lay claim to a legal type of their own.'

Flint snorted, not much mollified. 'When's this personalized brief likely to get here then?'

'He's not, not unless he's needed.'

'Oh?'

'Like I said, we can't charge her with anything and Fergus Maltham knows it. He's just got help on standby.'

'And meantime?'

'Meantime, I'm keeping them on ice until the warrant's passed and we've done a search of their van. Then, well, I see no option but to let Cassie Maltham go back there.'

Flint was frowning again, twisting his pen between his fingers and tapping alternate ends on the desk.

Mike watched the familiar action. It was one of Flint's strange affectations that he had an old-fashioned blotter on his desk-top, despite the fact he never used anything but a common-or-garden ball-point. Usually someone else's.

'What about hypnosis? If the memory really is lost . . . If she's not making a convenience out of it.'

'Already thought of that. It seems this Doctor Lucas has used it with Cassie before.'

'Cassie?' Flint said disapprovingly. He preferred formality, saw the use of first names as a sign of laxity.

'Mrs Maltham,' Mike corrected himself. 'Our lot suggest we wait for her and discuss it. Apparently Mrs Maltham's likely to respond better to someone she knows and trusts.'

Flint laughed harshly. 'I damn well bet she is.'

'Any attempt would be witnessed, of course.'

'Damn right it will be.' He frowned intently at Mike. 'The child. You say her story's the same. No chance the two of them . . .'

'You think the child's been hiding out somewhere with Cassie Maltham's help?' He sounded contemptuous, modified his tone, realizing that Flint was only trying on ideas for size. Wasn't that what Mike himself had been doing for the last few days? 'No, sir,' he said. 'I don't think so. I don't have an explanation.' He paused again. 'The hospital's running every test they can think of, if the child was drugged we should know fairly soon. If that's the case, well, when we know what was used that might give us some sort of lead.'

Flint nodded. 'Hmm. Maltham. He's some kind of chemistry teacher?'

Mike saw where he was leading. 'Combined Science I believe it is now, but that's pushing things a bit, sir.'

'Maybe, maybe. Note it anyway.'

'Yes, sir.'

'What exactly does the child remember?'

'As I said, nothing really. She keeps talking about a dark place and a woman's voice, but she can't recall any words. She says she was scared. Understandably so. Then this hand came out of the dark, she took it and found herself sitting between Cassie Maltham and a dead body on top of Tan's hill.'

Flint snorted again. It seemed to be his day for odd noises. 'Very Biblical,' he commented scornfully. 'A mystic hand reaching into the darkness and pulling her out.' He shook his head wearily. 'And that's pretty much what the Maltham woman says too? That she found herself in some dark hole of a place, saw a hand, reached out and grabbed it and Bingo! Whammy, one Sara Jane Cassidy mystically produced on the hill top. Good God, Mike! We'll be getting stone tablets and burning bushes soon.'

Mike smiled wryly. 'I expect the Cassidys are quite accepting of any miracle that's given them their child back.'

He hadn't been prepared for the sadness in his own voice, realized that Flint was looking sharply at him and saw his superior nod slowly.

'Far as that goes, Mike, I'm quite happy to accept

the miracle too. Thought by now we'd be looking for . . . Mike, it must have been hard on you, a case like this.' He paused as Mike's face hardened. Not the most perceptive of men, but even so, Flint nevertheless realized he might have trespassed too far this time. He tried again. 'I know about your son, of course, I just—'

'Yes, sir. Thank you.' Mike cut him off sharply. There were very few people he could talk to about Stevie, and Flint certainly wasn't on his list.

'Right. Well, then.' Flint began to sort through papers once more, putting rank between them once again. 'You'll brief me when this Doctor Lucas has shown herself and the path. reports begin to come in.'

'Yes, sir.' Mike rose to leave. Flint was already pretending he had left. Mike opened the door, slipped through and let it clang noisily behind him. Reluctantly, he decided to try and coax more out of Cassie Maltham.

There was one other odd bit of information that Bill had given him and that had confirmed one of Cassie's stranger assertions. The child, Sara, had been dressed, not in her own clothes, but in blue shorts and a yellow shirt obviously meant for a child somewhat taller than she was.

'Suzie was dressed like that,' Cassie had said. 'Didn't you look at her clothes? Even the shoes Sara was wearing. They were fastened up but still nearly dropped off her feet.'

'What are you getting at?' Mike had asked her.

'They're Suzie's clothes. Suzie's shoes. Not Sara Jane's.'

At the time it had seemed so absurd that, although of course it was on the recording of the interview, Mike had given it little further thought. Then Bill's phone call.

'There's a funny thing, Mike,' he'd said. 'The little girl, when she was found, well, it wasn't her clothes she was wearing. The shoes are too big for one thing.' He'd paused as though uncertain whether or not to give Mike the next bit. Then, 'Tell you another funny thing, Mike. Tynan says they match what Suzie Ashmore was wearing the day she went missing. They've gone to the lab, but we're wondering . . .' He hadn't bothered to elaborate, didn't need to. Layer upon layer, this case got more dementedly complex, more absurdly balanced on coincidence. There were times, Mike thought, when the whole thing seemed so bizarre it made the weirder cuttings in Tynan's old books look, by comparison, almost desirably sane.

Chapter Fourteen

Simon edged the car forward again, muttering irritably under his breath.

Each day since they'd left Fergus and Cassie, he and Anna had scoured every news programme they could get access to for news of the case; bought more newspapers in those few days than they normally read in a month, and Fergus had phoned them daily from the call box outside the village.

Fergus, they suspected, had told them only a fraction of what was going on. He'd been so evidently worried about Cassie, so reluctant to give specific details, that their already well-stoked imaginations had filled the void with wilder and wilder speculations.

Then this morning, seeing the live newscasts – Cassie and the little girl walking together from the entrance to the Greenway – there was no way that either could spend another day not knowing. Simon had phoned into work saying that they were both sick.

'We saw the news as well,' the secretary told him. Simon could feel her bristling attention, her readiness to interrogate.

'Well, tell him something,' he said, meaning his boss. 'I'll sort it when I get back.'

They'd driven non-stop. Non-stop until now, that was. The village streets, usually practically empty of anything but the odd pedestrian, were choked, and spluttered on an overdose of people, cameras, police and newsmen.

'Looks like a frigging film set.' Simon tried to edge forward again. 'I mean, look at them all. Where the hell did they all come from?'

'Try to back off. We'll cut down the other way,' Anna suggested. The milling crowd was pushing against the car, people bending to try and peer in at the window. A uniformed policeman appeared, gesturing at them to go back.

'What the hell's he think I'm trying to do?' Simon complained, jerking the car into reverse gear and trying to back through the people already closed in behind them. They began to move, slowly, the crowd parting reluctantly to let them by. In his mirror, Simon could see the officer gesturing, guiding them backwards, then pointing to a farm gate which would allow them space to turn. Simon, still grumbling irritably, followed his lead and reversed into the opening.

The officer appeared suddenly at the side of their car.

'It's the Thomases, isn't it?'

Simon frowned, wondering vaguely how he knew. Anna remembered though.

'Oh,' she said, 'you're the one who came to the cottage that morning.'

'Yes, Mrs Thomas, that's right.'

153

JANE ADAMS

Anna was about to continue when Simon cut in.
'What the hell's going on here, looks like a flying circus.
Can't you keep it under control?' Simon hated disorder
of any kind, especially when it interfered with the
smooth running of his day.

'We're doing our best, sir.' The young man sounded
aggrieved. 'But it's a public street. We can hardly call a
curfew, now can we, sir.'

'No, no, of course you can't,' Anna said quickly and
placatingly, casting a frosty look at Simon. 'We were
trying to get up onto the headland, to the Malthams.
They're in a caravan up there . . .'

'Yes, I know, Miss, but you'll not find them there
right now.'

'Oh?'

'No, Miss, they went with everyone back to Divisional HQ in Norwich.' He hesitated for a moment,
then said, 'You know the little girl's been found?'

'Yes, we saw it on the news. I mean, that's why
we've come down now, instead of tomorrow. We just
wanted . . .' She trailed off, looking back at the crowd.
She continued, suddenly slightly embarrassed, 'I guess
that's why all these others are here?'

The constable nodded. 'I expect it is.'

Anna smiled a little sheepishly. 'We'd just been so
worried, you see. We—'

Simon cut in sharply, in no mood to appease
authority.

'When will the Malthams be back?' His voice sharp
almost to the point of rudeness.

154

'Simon!'

The constable's face hardened, his whole body stiffened with official indignation. 'I wouldn't know, sir. No doubt when they've answered all of DI Croft's questions.'

He began to head back towards his official attempts to keep order.

Simon tapped irritably at the steering wheel.

'You didn't need to be rude to him,' Anna said.

'I wasn't rude.'

'No?'

She let it drop. Simon wasn't exactly in the mood for debate, particularly about himself.

'So what now?' she asked.

'We find somewhere for lunch and we think about it.'

He slammed the car into first and hit the accelerator hard enough for the engine to scream protest.

'. . . Interview resumed at two-sixteen p.m. Those present, Mrs Cassandra Maltham, Detective Inspector Michael Croft and WPC Saunders.' Mike looked thoughtfully at the hunched figure of the young woman seated at the table. 'Would you like some more tea, Mrs Maltham?'

She shook her head without even looking up. 'I want to see my husband.'

'He's outside, Mrs Maltham. I'll bring him in shortly.' He paused, crossed to the table, glancing over at the female officer seated by the door. There was no mistaking the disapproval in her look. Cassie Maltham had been growing more and more withdrawn. This last hour particularly, she had become visibly distressed, exhausted by what she so evidently saw as his meaningless questions. Mike sat down.

'Cassie, listen to me. I want you to go through this with me just one more time.'

'I've already told you all I can, all I know.' Her voice sounded dull, uncaring, all sparkle gone from it. She couldn't even be bothered to sound angry any more.

'Humour me. Tell me again. One last time.'

The door opened and a constable handed the WPC a note, she brought it over to Mike. So, the Lucas woman had arrived, had she. Well, she could damn well wait.

'Just one more time, Cassie.' He softened his voice a little, coaxing.

'I've already told you.' This time her voice was barely above a whisper. She looked up at him, though, and Mike felt a moment of shock at how pale she looked. He felt a sudden surge of anger. What was he doing to this woman? What evidence had he that she had committed any sort of crime?

Sharply he reminded himself that she could merely be very clever, a skilled manipulator, totally unscrupulous. But somehow, looking at her like this, the very thoughts took on the absurdity of black comedy. He sighed.

'Doctor Lucas is here. Will you tell her what happened?' He'd spoken this time with conscious gentleness as though speaking to a hurt child, saw the WPC's face and her disgust that he could be so downright patronizing, but Cassie nodded, eyes suddenly welling with tears.

'All right,' she said. 'I'll tell her.'

Croft rose from his seat and strode impatiently over to the door, shouted for someone to bring Mr Maltham and Dr Lucas into the interview room. He was well and truly sick of this whole thing, wanted nothing so much as to write up his report – fun reading that was going to be – and head for somewhere he could get a decent meal and a night's sleep. Despite the fact that it was not yet even mid-afternoon, he felt he'd worked a double shift since that morning. Looking at her, he figured Cassie must feel the same.

He stood aside to allow Fergus Maltham and the doctor to come in. Fergus, blazingly angry, every instinct screaming to protect, crossed straight to his wife, gathering her to him. Croft turned away irritably, took a look at Dr Lucas, then took a second look and extended a hand. 'I'm DI Croft,' he said. 'Mike Croft.'

She took the proffered hand with a wry smile, obviously used to the double take. Tall, black, elegant; he would guess she got a lot of men looking twice at her. Mike wasn't certain what he had expected Dr Maria Lucas to be, but it certainly wasn't this.

She released his hand, and went over to the Malthams. 'Cassie? Hi there.'

Cassie looked up and managed a half smile.

Mike felt suddenly that he'd been usurped.

Maria Lucas reached across, commandeered the other chair and seated herself close to Cassie, taking her hands. 'Now, what the hell have you been doing, sweetheart? You going to tell me about it?'

Her voice was soft but very clear. Educated, but the English wasn't clipped or overformalized, tempered instead by a rhythmic quality. Like a story-teller, Mike thought. It was the kind of voice you wanted to listen to.

'Hey,' she went on, gesturing at the recorder, 'do you think we can have that thing off?'

Mike shook his head and Cassie put in, 'I said I'd go through things with you here. Said I'd tell him what happened again.' Her voice sounded small and brittle, rising querulously. 'But I've told him everything, told him over and over again and I don't know what else to say.' She broke off, sobbing. Fergus moved to comfort her again and Dr Lucas awarded Mike a cool and disapproving look.

'Hardly standard procedure, is it, Inspector?'

'It's hardly a standard case.' He was losing her, he realized. The last thing he wanted was this woman as his enemy. She would, he sensed, make a very efficient adversary should it come to that.

He sighed, his tone placatory this time. 'Doctor Lucas, all I'm trying to establish are the facts. All you're trying to do is get to the truth of what Cassie's been through. Do we have to fight over this?'

'My concern, Mr Croft, is for my patient. That, first and foremost.' She gave him a long cold look, then turned her attention once more back to Cassie. 'Now, how about we start with waking up this morning?'

Simon glanced irritably around the small crowded interior of the bar. They'd driven in a wide circle, ending up only a village away from their original destination and finally taken a chance on this local watering hole simply because it advertised pub food.

This wasn't one of the tourist pubs on the coast. It was, when they got inside, crowded with locals who looked askance at these two strangers. Simon was hopeless in these situations. He just glared at everyone, gave back questioning gaze for questioning gaze. Anna had hustled him into a corner where he could cause as little damage as possible to public relations and made her way to the bar, wondering for the umpteenth time how anyone like Simon – who earned his living charming complete strangers into parting with departmental cash – could be so socially inept off-duty.

She smiled warmly at the landlord, made a point of answering his questions about where they'd come from and of asking his advice on what to order. Within moments she was involved in barside conversation, exchanging smiles. Simon, watching with a mix of pride and disapproval, shook his head. As PA to one of their companies chief execs, Anna spent most of her life smoothing feathers and building bridges. Most of the time she did it set on automatic.

Bringing their drinks, she made her way back to their table.

'Food'll be about ten minutes,' she told him, smiling,

a personal smile this time, not her official one. She set
their drinks down and reached for his hand. For several
minutes they sat in silence, listening to the ebb and
flow of conversation around them. Cigarette smoke
drifted over, mingling with odd words, phrases, just as
troublesome, just as ephemeral.

'They were talking about Cassie,' Anna told him.

'Who?' His voice was sharp.

'The men at the bar. Don't worry. I just said we were
passing through, going to Norwich.'

'I'm not worried,' he retorted crossly. Then, 'What
were they saying?'

'Wondering whether she was mixed up in it. If what
the papers said was true.'

She didn't need to elaborate.

'Her mother wants hanging saying all that,' Simon
muttered angrily. 'I mean, as if Cassie hasn't been
through enough already.'

'I never met her mother. Fergus says she's evil.'

'Candidate for burning if ever I met one.'

Anna raised her eyebrows. He went on, defensively,
'You've not met her. That woman is warped. Poor kid,
whatever she said or did her mother would twist it to
mean something else. I don't wonder her father left
them, just a shame he didn't take Cassie along too.
Never thought she'd do a thing like that though. I
mean to sell out your own kid like that, just isn't human
somehow.'

Anna sipped her drink slowly, then spoke cautiously.
'You don't think she could have anything to do with

all this . . . Cassie I mean?' Simon was glaring at her.
'Simon, I don't mean she'd do anything willingly, not
to hurt anyone, never mind a child, but, but maybe,
bringing her back here to where her cousin disappeared, couldn't it be all too much for her, make her
do things and then forget them? Really forget them, I
mean.'

He stared hard at her. 'I can't believe you're saying
this, Anna.' He waited for her denial. It didn't come.
'You really think she masterminded the whole thing,
do you, managed to be with us on the beach while her
mystery accomplice snatched Sara? Managed to play
the innocent all the time the world and his wife were
searching for her, played the game while Janice Cassidy
cried on her shoulder then made some crazy arrangement with this mystery accomplice to produce the child
out of nowhere in front of the world's press?' He
paused then added, 'Or you think maybe she got that
poor woman to do the kidnapping for her, then beat
her to death and pretended to find the child?'

He saw the hurt in her eyes, saw tears before she
looked swiftly away from him, and felt immediate
remorse.

'Hey, look, love, I'm sorry. I know you didn't mean
it like that.'

She made no answer. Looking closer he realized
that she was crying, tears dripping slowly onto the
tabletop, splashing into her drink.

'Hey, Anna.' He shifted round, dragging his chair
to sit beside her, fumbled in his pocket for a handker-

chief that he knew wouldn't be there. 'Look,' he said, trying to make amends, 'you'll make your drink salty. Save it for the food, we might need it then.'

'Oh, Simon. I don't mean anything bad about Cassie. I love her too, you know that.'

'I know, and I'm sorry too. Both been on edge, haven't we?'

The food arrived then, the landlord's wife bustling around the table. Simon did his best to be polite, and shield Anna from too much attention. The fact was, he knew exactly how she felt. These last few days trying to function normally when their thoughts were so much elsewhere; this feeling of being both involved and excluded. Then too, Anna hadn't been very well this week. Some sort of mild bug, probably, or just a reaction to the stress making her slightly sick. He looked more closely at her, a thought suddenly striking at him.

'What are you drinking?'

She looked up, surprised and, oddly, guilty. 'Orange juice. Why?'

'Just orange juice . . . Anna, been a bit slow off the mark again, haven't I?'

She nodded, slowly. 'I don't know for certain yet, but . . .'

'Then it's time we did know. Come on, eat up then we'll get going.'

'Going where?'

'First, we find a chemist, got to be one locally big enough to sell one of those pregnancy test things. Then we go to Norwich, to Police headquarters or whatever they call it. Find out what they're doing to Cassie.'

She laughed, life suddenly feeling very good, her natural optimism coming to the fore once again. 'I don't suppose they're doing anything to Cassie, but yes, we'll do both of those things.' She began to eat, suddenly relieved, then she said, shyly, 'I've been so afraid, you know?'

'What of? Telling me? No, I don't want to know if it's the postman's . . .'

She laughed. 'Fool.' She shook her head. 'No, not of telling you, at least, sort of that too but that's just me being daft.'

'I'll say it is.' He paused, looked at her, realizing suddenly that what she wanted to say was somehow, not easy.

'It's just that, all this happening, somehow, I keep feeling that the baby is all bound up with it too. I keep thinking that something bad's going to happen.' She looked at him, willing him to tell her that it was imagination, that it was quite common for pregnant women to have strange ideas. 'Try turning it around.' He spoke quietly. 'See it as something positive.'

'What do you mean?'

He shrugged, not sure how to put it into words. 'I don't know really. It's just that so many bad things have happened you're almost bound to think only bad things can happen. But there's no way this can be a bad thing. This baby. Our baby.' He paused, smiled, repeated the words. 'Our baby was like as

163

not conceived here. It's like a promise, a making right somehow, turning something good from all the dark things that have happened.' He smiled at her, reached for her hand. 'Hey! You're crying again!'

'Sorry.'

'What for?' He squeezed her hand warmly. 'Now, eat. We've got a lot to do. We've got to find out if you're telling me the truth or not.'

'Fool,' Anna told him once more, but she smiled, feeling better than she had in days.

'Mr and Mrs Thomas are here, sir. They want to know about Mrs Maltham.'

Croft glanced up at the officer standing a little uncertainly in the doorway of Flint's office.

'Well,' Flint commented, 'since they're here they can save us the trouble of taking the Malthams back to the van. Tell them DI Croft will be down shortly,' he then turned his attention back to Mike. 'The search revealed nothing?'

'No, but then we'd little expectation that it would. Fergus Maltham didn't object, neither did he take up his right to be there.'

'Hardly likely to, was he?' Flint said wryly. 'Not when you had his wife here.'

'Quite.'

'So where does that leave us?'

'Well, we've got the child back.'

'Though God alone knows how. To say nothing of

now having a murder on our hands. 'So what does this Lucas woman have to say? She willing to use hypnosis is she?'

Having Flint talk about Maria Lucas as this 'Lucas woman' seemed dreadfully inappropriate somehow, but Mike said nothing. 'Yes, she's agreed. Cassie Maltham's willing to give it a try. The Doctor's persuaded her she may be hiding something from herself. Something she saw, maybe, that brought back memories of the childhood trauma and she buried it without being aware. Apparently it can happen that way, it can then go on to affect anything connected with that incident. Episodes of amnesia that seem unrelated but in fact have the same trigger.' He shrugged. 'It's foreign ground to me, but if it gives us answers.'

'Hmm.' Flint sounded far from convinced. 'Well, we must be seen to be doing all we can.' He paused, his mind evidently shifting elsewhere. 'What do you make of those phone calls?' he asked, referring to surprise information from the two women who had earlier reported on the itinerant woman they'd looked for.

'I'd say they make a kind of sense. Both women saw the itinerant clearly, even spoke to her. If they believe that the picture of Mrs Maltham's dream woman is a picture of the itinerant we've been looking for then I say we should accept it as far as it goes. One thing though, sir, I'd rather we didn't leak that to the press until after Doctor Lucas's session with Cassie tomorrow. I'd like to see if she can dig up any link first.'

'Agreed. We'll do what we can to keep the hat c
until then.' Flint dropped the ever-present pen dow
onto the redundant blotter, rubbed his face with h
hands and screwed his fists in an almost childlil
gesture into tired eyes. 'Hospital and Path. repor
aren't all in yet. The kiddie's been found and the bo
isn't going anywhere. I suggest you make an early d
of it.'

Mike rose. 'Yes, sir.' Early? He was hardly doir
short time, though compared to the fourteen- or fiftee
hour stretches, minimum, he'd been putting in, l
supposed it qualified. He'd arranged to meet Bill ar
Tynan later anyway.

He took his leave of Flint, and went down to h
office to collect the latest batch of telephone calls tl
case had generated. There were two more calle
connecting the woman drawn from Cassie's drea
with an 'old tramp' as one called her, 'a gypsy' anoth
said. Both sightings were within a ten-mile radius
the village. There were two 'psychics' proclaiming th
they had messages from the woman in the pictur
messages from beyond the grave. 'More right tha
they know,' Mike muttered to himself. Others, mo
innocent, from people who thought they'd seen som
thing relevant and a couple telling of legends, smu
glers' tunnels leading from the cliffs inland to Tan's h
and the local church.

Mike dropped the messages back on his desk, ar
made his way down to the station office. To his surpris
Maria Lucas was there, perched contentedly on one

the desks, drinking coffee and chatting to the duty officer.

'Doctor Lucas, I thought you'd be long gone. The Malthams, have they left with their friends?'

'They did.' She still sounded somewhat irritated. Then she smiled, 'I wanted a word before you left. Got a minute?'

He nodded. 'Look I was just leaving . . .'

'Then we'll talk over dinner, if it's not too early for you?'

Mike gave her a surprised look. Her direct, confident manner took him aback, made him feel like some inept schoolboy, a feeling not helped by seeing the duty officer smirking at him. He held the door for her, watching appreciatively as she slid off the desk and picked up her coat and bag.

'Thank you. A gentleman as well.'

He winced at the sarcasm, then scowled at the loud guffaw of the duty sergeant and shut the door, firmly.

'Are you always this forthright?' he asked.

She raised her eyebrows in exaggerated surprise. 'Detective Inspector Croft, I'm asking you to discuss business with me over dinner, not book a double room at the local hotel. Now let's go to my car.'

He paused with his hand on the car door handle. 'There's something I have to clear up before we go anywhere,' he said.

She shook her head. 'Don't worry about it. Cassie tells me you've been very understanding under the circumstances. Believe me, she wants this sorted as

much as you do. If there's a chance she's guilty o
something then the sooner we know the sooner sh
can be helped.'

'And if I ask you questions about her?'

'I'll answer what I can. We've agreed that, Inspecto
Croft.'

'Mike.'

'Mike. It's hard to explain what it's like for someon
like Cassie. She thought she was getting better, living
so-called normal life. Then something like this come
along and the rug is well and truly pulled from unde
her feet. Now, she could take it one of two ways. Sh
could either opt out in some way, maybe even fu
retreat, she's done it before. Or she could take th
option she's chosen this time. Face whatever come
and deal with it. It's a very courageous stance to take
A year ago, I don't think she'd have had any choice
She'd have just overloaded and sunk back again int
some form of psychosis. She's come a long way. I war
to make sure she's vindicated. You understand that?'

He nodded. 'Essentially we want the same thing. T
get to the bottom of what has affected Cassie so badly

'Right,' she acknowledged. 'Now let's go eat.'

Mike drove the winding route to Tynan's cotta
feeling more relaxed than he had done in months. A
it happened, they had discussed almost everything b
the 'Cassie dilemma' as Maria called it. They ha
agreed on almost nothing, argued vociferously an

laughed too loudly. Mike felt that a whole lifetime of grief and mourning had begun to lift. Not that it was a lifetime, of course, he thought. Just that sometimes it felt that way.

He'd left her at her hotel and walked back to his car. She'd called after him that she'd enjoyed the evening, that they must do it again.

'Do you mean that?' he'd asked her, 'or are you just being polite.'

She'd grinned at him, then laughed aloud. 'I'm never just polite.'

Tynan let him in to the familiar cottage, waved him through to the living room and followed shortly after with the tea. Bill was already sprawled comfortably, eyes half-closed, in one of the ageing chintz-covered armchairs.

'Evening, Mike.'

Croft lowered himself gingerly into what was fast becoming his chair, the one with the rockers that misbehaved at the slightest wrong move.

'Pleasant meal?' Bill opened his eyes, looked sideways at Mike, who snorted in amusement.

'News certainly gets around. I take it you called at the office?'

Tynan handed him his tea.

'How's Sara?' Mike asked them.

'In a lot better shape than her mum and dad,' Tynan told him. 'They're keeping her in overnight but she's well enough to be starving and demanding chocolate. Shaky of course, but taking it all remarkably well.'

He sounded concerned about that, Mike thought. 'It's probably going to catch up with her later, once the excitement dies down.'

Bill nodded. 'That's what the doctors are saying. You know the Cassidys would like to go away for a few days. I've told them there would be no objections?'

Mike shook his head. 'None. If the child's told us all she can there's no need for them to stay around needlessly. You've made sure they leave a contact address though?'

'Sure, going to Mrs C's mum's. The address and number's in the records.'

Mike sipped his tea, slowly. 'She remembered anything more?'

Bill shook his head. 'Nothing. The report I sent over earlier is about it really. The kid has no idea of what happened in the last five days. She remembers someone calling her name, went up the path and then began to climb the hill, then, nothing, apart from hearing a woman's voice, but she's no idea of what was said or even of how often or when she heard it. She said it was like being half-asleep.'

'All of the time?' Mike asked. 'No, that doesn't make sense. She didn't starve for those five days, she must have eaten, must have drunk and no one goes five days without pissing. She remembers nothing like that?'

Tynan shook his head. 'Nothing definite. The hospital's been looking at the drugs angle. There are traces of something which could be narcotic. They don't have

170

the specialist knowledge here so they've sent samples off to the poisons unit, see what they turn up, but it could be a day or two longer.'

'When are we likely to have the path. reports on the body?'

'Tomorrow, with luck. They're giving it priority.' Bill nodded thoughtfully. 'Never seen such a bloody mess. It was as though someone set out to break every bone in the woman's body.'

'Not the face though,' Mike said. It was something that had struck him at the time. The body had been beaten so badly that in places it resembled butcher's meat; yet the face was virtually untouched, superficial bruising at the temples, but nothing more. It was as though whoever killed her was determined that she be identifiable still. It made about as much sense as anything else did.

'They hazarded yet how long she's been dead?' Tynan asked.

Mike shrugged. 'No time at all. They're not willing to commit until the autopsy's complete, but she was still warm when we got there.' He frowned angrily. 'We could have been not a hundred yards away when it happened.'

'So,' Tynan enquired, 'why didn't you hear anything? Didn't she cry out?'

'Who knows, but the hill itself would muffle sound, and if she was hit on the head first . . . I noticed bruising on the right temple, almost the only mark on the face though.'

Mike paused, went off on a different tack. 'You say the child's been eating?'

Bill nodded. 'Yes, ravenous. The doctors don't think she's been given much, a little milk maybe.' He paused, added by way of explanation, 'She threw up all over the consultant.' He smiled, vaguely approving and went on, 'If she was drugged I suppose it would have suppressed her appetite as well as making her hard to feed.'

'Near impossible, I'd have thought, though I suppose there would be times when the sedation was lighter and she'd have been able to swallow.'

'So,' Mike said, 'the drugs could have suppressed her appetite?'

'But not emptied her bladder for her,' Bill added.

Mike gave him a wry look. 'I figure these things probably don't wait for a convenient moment. If the girl was drugged, she'd simply have wet herself.'

'In which case, someone changed her clothes only a little while before she was found.'

'Oh?' Mike enquired.

'The child's clothes were dry and clean. I asked the lab to test, there was nothing.'

'No smell either,' Tynan said thoughtfully. 'She'd have been pretty high by the time we'd got to her.'

Mike nodded. The same thoughts had passed through his own mind. 'Any clue as to where she was kept?'

Bill shook his head. 'The report, such as it is, you'll find on your desk, but for what it's worth there were fragments of dried leaves clinging to the shirt. Mud stains, wet ones, on the shorts, but those could have come from the hill.' He sighed. 'Again, we're waiting on reports.'

Mike thought for a moment, then asked, 'You heard about the phone calls connecting the dream woman to the itinerant we were looking for?'

Bill nodded. 'I read the day book. There were two more after you left, came in just before I got back. Looks promising. By the way, how did you make out with the shrink?'

Mike frowned slightly. Spoke more curtly than he'd intended. 'She's being helpful.' He frowned more deeply as he intercepted a knowing glance between Tynan and Bill. He put his cup down, stretched, decided it was time to leave. They could achieve little more tonight.

'Want to stay over?' Tynan asked. Mike shook his head.

'Thanks, but I want to make an early start.'

Bill gave him a speculative look which Mike deliberately ignored. 'I think we should all get some sleep,' he said. 'I don't even know if this will still be my case tomorrow.'

Bill suddenly sobered, nodded slowly. It had been almost chance that Mike had been placed in charge of the enquiry so far. He'd been in the right place at the right time, but now they had a murder enquiry going it was unlikely the specialists would keep their noses out for much longer.

He rose slowly to his feet, suddenly feeling his age and joined Mike in bidding John Tynan good night. Tomorrow could bring a lot of changes.

Chapter Fifteen

Mike stifled a yawn. He had in fact managed very little sleep. His head was stuffed too full of random thoughts and speculations for him to sink long into oblivion.

When, finally, he had managed to force his body into sleep his mind seemed determined to defy him. He'd dreamed. Dreamed of Tan's hill and the Greenway, walked up the steep sides of the hill, grown more steep, more slippery than reality, as dream images do, fought his way to the top to be confronted by some scene from a maniac's nightmare. Figures cavorting in some obscene dance, their naked bodies gleaming in the moonlight, blood dripping from deep cuts as they hacked and beat at their own bodies with long-handled knives. In his dream he had tried to run, but the figures saw him, tearing and cutting at his clothing, pulling him to the ground. He'd opened his mouth, tried to scream, but the figures cast him down with as little effort as they would have needed to lift a child. The knives came closer, he could feel the coldness of metal against his flesh, felt a sudden absurd remorse at all the paperwork his murder would leave Bill.

A long blade of shining steel lowered slowly towards his face. He looked up, knowing a moment of complete terror when he realized that the hand holding it was John Tynan's. The knife moved closer, blade flicking lightly against his cheeks, a sudden and painful slicing of the flesh before it lifted again, this time dripping with his blood. Mike stared in horror at the steel gleaming gently in the soft moonlight. There was something inscribed on the blade, something he could just make out if he stared hard, forced his vision past its normal limits. He had the sudden overwhelming conviction that if he could only read the words, then these insane celebrants would have to set him free. That his magic would prove stronger than theirs. He peered harder, struggling to make out the strange, writhing symbols engraved deep in the blade of the knife.

'Oh, my God.' Stupid or what. Mike laughed aloud, fear suddenly dissipating as he read the 'magical' inscription. 'Eversharp. Ten year guarantee', with the company logo emblazoned proudly alongside. He woke then, bedclothes tangled around him and soaked with sweat. He lay back, laughing at himself, but, by the same token, reached out and turned on the bedside lamp, unable completely to eliminate the cold dread that had seemed ready to choke the life from him.

He'd been unable to sleep again, instead he had changed his soaked sheets and forced down several cups of strong coffee. Then he'd taken himself straight in to work and waited for the pathology and forensic reports to come in.

They made interesting reading.

Bill arrived just as he was reaching the end. 'Tell us anything?'

'Lots of things I didn't want to know,' Croft said wryly.

'Oh?' He sat himself down comfortably. 'Care to give me a summary or do I have to wade through for myself?'

Mike smiled, said he thought he could just about manage to summarize. 'The clothes the child was wearing – the store labels were still in. Big chain-store as it turns out and it's a matter of policy to keep design records.'

'Suzanne Ashmore's?'

'That's taking a leap, Bill. What we do know is that they are contemporary and identical.' He paused. 'The mother's seen them, Suzanne's mother that is. She confirms that her daughter was dressed, if not in these, then at least in clothing like it.' He hesitated, glanced up at Bill. 'The shoes are a different story. It seems that in term-time Suzie Ashmore had to wear indoor shoes at school. Nothing special, just plimsolls or canvas ones like these. Her mother wrote her name in them. But then, you saw the shoes, you know that.'

Bill nodded slowly. 'Suzie's name was in the shoes, but on its own . . .'

'Well, the name, as you saw, had been worn away by wearing them, but Mrs Ashmore is convinced that it's her writing. What clinches it, maybe, is that Suzie herself wrote her class number in red actually inside the shoe. You probably missed that. The shoe would

177

have to be unlaced before you could see it.'

'Someone else could have known that.'

'Devil's advocate doesn't suit you, Bill,' Croft commented. 'No, what it points to is that someone kept the clothing for all this time, that someone is almost certainly Suzie Ashmore's abductor, probably more than that.'

'But what doesn't make sense is why now? Why does someone commit a crime like this and keep such damning evidence, then wait twenty years to commit another?' He frowned. 'The link has to be Cassie Maltham. Her coming back here. Someone knew.'

'Or Cassie Maltham herself? Or are you discounting her now, Bill?'

'No, I'm not. I'd be far happier if she had an alibi of some sort, something we could test, but this memory-lapse business . . . too convenient by half if you ask me.'

They fell silent for a moment, trying to make some sense of what they knew, then Mike roused himself. 'OK, let's take the most extreme position. Cassie Maltham's some kind of nut who engineered the disappearance of her cousin twenty years ago.'

'Motive?'

'God knows. Jealousy. Suzie had everything she wanted. Security, attention, freedom that she certainly didn't have. Maybe, in some roundabout way, she thought that by getting cousin Suzie out of the picture she could have all of those things.'

'Sounds a bit far-fetched,' Bill said, frowning.

'Like I said, the most extreme case. But, she has guilt feelings that cause her maybe to block out what really happened then. At first she makes up some sort of explanation and the story becomes so real she can't tell truth from lies any more.' He looked at Bill, smiled. 'How am I doing?'

Bill declined to comment. Instead, he pressed the intercom and asked for coffee to be sent in.

Mike continued. 'Coming back here triggered the original memories, made it harder to hide behind the lies she'd been telling herself—'

'So she kidnaps another child, drugs her, hides her God alone knows where, then dresses her in Suzie's clothes that she's kept hidden dry and freshly aired somewhere just for such an occasion and produces her on cue in front of a dozen astounded witnesses? Just in time to get on the live newscast at eight-fifteen? Come on, Mike. I may think Cassie Maltham's a bit touched but I can't swallow that, not even as a wild theory. Think of the organization involved, the planning. Apart from anything else she'd have needed to come down here before this holiday of theirs, find somewhere to hide the kid away, equip herself with whatever Sara Jane was drugged with . . . What was it by the way? Path. boys know yet?'

'Not for certain. They're convinced it's plant based and of a group related to the digitoxins. They found traces of alkaloids and Sara was found to have a minor kidney inflammation. Nothing serious but it's a common side-effect of many alkaloids.'

'Thought they were poisons.'

'They are, in the right dosages. The lab boys seem to think that whoever administered the drug knew what they were doing.'

'I don't know much about this, but I remember reading, or seeing it on telly maybe, that a lot of common plants have some narcotic effects.'

Mike nodded. 'Lettuce contains a small quantity of digitalis, so do foxgloves, of course, then there's belladonna, common bindweed and jimson weed.'

'Never heard of that one.'

'It isn't native, it's an escapee from botanical gardens and the like. Ugly-looking, prickly thing. My ex-father-in-law found some growing in his garden and looked it up. I believe it's only just this side of legal.'

'Oh, but they can't tell us any more?'

Mike shook his head. 'Not yet. The autopsy on the woman's not a lot of help.'

'What's it do? Tell us she was battered to death?'

Mike laughed briefly. 'Something like that.' He leaned back in his chair as the coffee arrived. They'd given him a new office chair, an irritating, swivelling affair on castors that resisted all his attempts to lean backwards. There was, he thought, something stupidly satisfying in seeing how far back on two legs a chair would lean before striking disaster.

The office door closed and he reached for his coffee. 'The blow that killed her wasn't the first, and certainly not the last. She'd been hit across the temples hard enough to stun but didn't die until her assailant smashed the back of her skull, severing the spinal cord at the same time.'

'Angle of attack?' Bill asked, sipping his coffee.

'That blow, behind, below and upward. Sounds awkward, almost as though the assailant was sitting or crouching on the ground when his victim tried to get up.'

'*His* victim.'

'The force of the blows would indicate considerable strength. Could have been a woman. I'm not wiping that one out, but the pathologist says that the fractures of the limbs came from a single blow each time. If she was stunned, she couldn't have put up much of a fight . . .'

'And if she was getting up or trying to when the killing blow was struck she must have still had the use of her legs, which means those injuries were probably caused post-mortem.'

'Path, lab thinks so too.'

'Hmm, so a man, or possibly a very strong or very angry woman. What does that discount, all children under sixteen and about another ten per cent of the population?'

'Something like that, though I'd drop the age limit.' He frowned thoughtfully. 'Funny thing is, Bill, she doesn't appear to have put up much of a fight. Nothing under the fingernails.'

'Can't scratch with your arms broken.'

Mike stared, appalled that he hadn't thought of that, appalled also at the chilling image they were discussing so evenly.

'She must have come from somewhere,' he said softly. Though if this woman and the female itinerant they had searched for were one and the same, it was possible that no one would have missed her. Only the nuisance factor of an old woman trying to sell clothes-pegs would be gone. Nothing more. It saddened him deeply.

'Dental records?' Bill's quiet voice brought him back to business.

'Not much sign that she's had work done.'

'Her blood group is A, just like about a third of the population and her estimated age late-fifties to early-sixties. Oh, and no children.'

'Motives for the attack,' Bill mused. 'Sexual?'

'No, not that we can tell. Or, at least, she wasn't raped, though what went through his mind, of course . . . It crossed my mind it might be revenge, but that doesn't fit in with the other factors, like her being found at the same time as Sara Jane.'

'Revenge? You mean, because it was known we were looking for her?'

Mike nodded. 'Could be someone decided she was guilty, and, as we didn't seem to be doing too good a job of finding her, decided to do it for us.'

'I don't see it. Vigilantes in the middle of rural Norfolk. You watch too much telly.'

'Yeah, maybe. Like I said, it doesn't fit with anything else anyway.'

'And no sign from anything of where Sara Jane was kept?'

Mike shook his head once more. 'Nothing helpful. Fragments of dried leaves clinging to her shirt and some traces of wet mud on her shorts, but the chances are both came from on the hill. She was sitting on the ground when we found her and it was still pretty damp that morning.'

Bill nodded. Nothing much there. 'When's this hypnosis malarkey supposed to be happening?' he asked abruptly.

'Eleven o'clock.'

'Think it will turn anything up?'

Mike shrugged. 'Who knows? We can but try.'

Cassie poked at the food Fergus had set in front of her. She'd slept badly and felt exhausted, strung tight, dreading the session with Dr Lucas that lay ahead of her.

She picked up her knife, rubbed irritably at an imagined speck of dirt, tried to eat, just to please Fergus.

Returning to the caravan the night before had seemed like just the continuation of her nightmare. Knowing that the place had been searched, that their things had been touched, pried at and poked into by hands of strangers, increased her sense of violation. It wasn't fair.

Worse, she and Fergus had argued, tensions having risen so high that Cassie couldn't help but lash out. She had raged at him for 'spoiling things' by insisting that they come back here. Screamed, cried, hurled insults and anything else she could find while Anna and Simon first tried to calm the situation and finally had simply looked on like embarrassed strangers caught up in some tragedy they had no part of.

Finally, she had calmed down enough to simply cry, deep, wrenching, selfish tears, but they had helped and her anger had dissipated enough for her to feel embarrassed and awkward even now.

Fergus said little. Simon and Anna talked, mostly to each other, with a determined brightness that made Cassie want to start screaming all over again. She gave up the pretence of trying to eat, lay down her fork and sat staring at the congealing egg like some mutinous child.

Fergus didn't even bother to try and cajole her into eating. Childishly, Cassie wanted him to, wanted attention. She flicked at the fork on her plate so that it clinked loudly against the china. No one took any notice so she did it again. Then she sighed, and asked herself just what sort of silly game she was playing.

'I'm sorry,' she said. She spoke softly, as though not wanting to be heard, but the conversation stopped and the attention of all three turned on her.

'For what?' Anna asked gently. 'Look, Cassie, you're entitled to get mad.'

'I didn't just get angry though, did I?' Somehow, Cassie wasn't yet ready to purge herself of all the self-pity she was feeling.

'It doesn't matter,' Simon told her. 'Consider it forgotten,' he continued expansively, irritating Cassie more than ever. She didn't want gentle, considered answers right now. She didn't know what she did want but it wasn't this.

Her thoughts, becoming more and more clouded, more and more self-flagellating, were interrupted by Simon speaking again.

'We've got something to tell you both,' he said. 'We would have told you last night, but, well, it didn't seem like good timing.'

Cassie looked up, paying more attention. It was clear though, from the look of suppressed excitement, that he wasn't thinking of her now.

'The fact is, well, we're pregnant.'

He said it with such a sense of profound satisfaction that even Cassie found herself jolted out of her destructive mood. Fergus, plainly every bit as delighted as Simon, was reaching over to congratulate them both and all three seemed to be talking at once. A jumble of pleasure and speculation and hopefulness.

Cassie watched them and felt suddenly left out, isolated from this ordinary world in which people did things like have babies and plan for the future. Her earlier mood of self-indulgent misery disappeared, to be replaced by something much deeper and more profound. A dreadful fear that this nightmare she was living through would go on for ever. That there would be no end to the persecution her own mind seemed set upon inflicting on her soul. She and Fergus had rarely

discussed having a family. There had been this tacit
agreement that too many things had to be ironed out
before they could take that further and, it seemed to
Cassie, final step.

They were looking at her expectantly, wanting to
involve her.

'Cassie?' Fergus said.

She managed to smile. 'It's wonderful,' she managed,
'just wonderful.' Then she burst into tears and rushed
from the room.

Mike had been astounded at how seemingly simple
and ordinary the whole procedure had been. Dr Lucas
had spent some time alone with Cassie, calming her
and talking the process through, then she'd allowed
Mike and Fergus back into the room and they had
watched as she talked Cassie down through deepening
levels of consciousness until she looked, to Mike, to be
in some kind of deep sleep.

He'd prepared a list of questions he needed answers
to, much to Maria Lucas's amusement. 'It doesn't work
quite like that, you know,' she'd told him. 'She's not
some medium getting messages from your Great-Aunt
Maud. We're trying to unlock the memories in Cassie's
subconscious, not invoke some mystic oracle.'

'Well, just try,' he'd said, smiling at her, trying to re-
create some of the easy intimacy they'd shared the
night before. Maria Lucas was having none of it. This
was business.

Cassie was speaking now, responding to Maria Lucas's instructions, describing that morning on the Greenway when Sara Jane had been found. She proceeded in a low, almost conversational tone, to explain how she had slipped away from Fergus while he was talking to the constable on duty. There was no mystery that time, they'd simply been too busy, one arguing, one giving official responses, to take any notice of her.

'Why was it so important you go to Tan's hill right then?' Maria Lucas asked her.

'I heard her calling to me.'

'Who, Cassie, who did you hear?'

'I heard Suzie. She was on the hill and she was calling to me.'

Dr Lucas exchanged a swift glance with Mike. She'd heard about the other morning, when Mike had found Cassie wandering and claiming to have heard Suzie calling.

Fergus was watching his wife intently. He looked strained, aged. Cassie was speaking again.

'I climbed the hill, but she wasn't there. I called out to her, but she didn't answer me, then I heard someone crying.'

Dr Lucas stopped her. 'Was it Suzie?'

'No. Not Suzie. A child crying. Not very loud. I thought she sounded hurt. I went to look.'

'Where did you look, Cassie?'

'I looked in the hidey hole.'

'The what!' Mike had been told to stay quiet, but he couldn't help himself.

187

Dr Lucas glared at him.

'Sorry,' he mouthed. 'Ask her.'

She gave him an impatient look. 'What hidey hole, Cassie?'

'In the hedges, near the bottom of the hill. I thought I couldn't get through, it was all overgrown, all brambles, but when I pushed they just seemed to fall apart. I reached in and she took my hand. I remember telling her it was all right and pulling the brambles apart with my other hand. It was hard to get back up the hill. I thought I heard someone calling me again, but it didn't matter then. I'd found Sara. That's why Suzie kept calling me, you see. To find Sara.'

'And you climbed back up the hill again? Cassie, can you answer me, sweetheart?' The Doctor waited for a moment, then she gently clasped Cassie's hand, looked at Mike. 'I think that's all we're going to get. I've been through these sessions before, get so far, then she seems to just shut down.'

'But we're getting somewhere!' Mike protested angrily. 'This, this hidey hole. Ask her where it is.'

Maria Lucas shook her head. 'No more,' she said softly, then as though to placate him. 'Ask her when she comes out of it. She may well remember parts consciously now, but like a dream. A bit fragmented.'

Mike sighed in exasperation, knowing there was nothing he could do. 'All right, all right. But I'll talk to her straight away.'

He could see Fergus preparing to argue. 'You can stay, Mr Maltham. This isn't a formal interview.' He could see that Fergus Maltham was far from happy with any of this but ignored him, turning instead to watch Dr Lucas ease Cassie gently from the hypnotic state, seeing her breathing deepen and her slow movements and relaxed expression, as though she'd just woken from deep sleep.

'How are you feeling' Maria Lucas asked.

Cassie appeared to consider for a moment, then she nodded. 'Better,' she said. 'Easier.'

'Good. You remember what you told me?'

Cassie frowned. Mike desperately resisted the temptation to prompt her, guide her memory into the paths he wanted it to follow.

'Some things. It's a bit hazy. There was a bramble patch.' She laughed suddenly. 'Or is that just my subconscious telling me I've been too prickly to get near lately?'

She was looking at Fergus as she said this, asking forgiveness for the way she'd behaved earlier. Mike saw Fergus's expression soften, his eyes crinkle at her as his mouth twitched at the corners. Impatience getting the better of him, he spoke more sharply than he'd intended.

'The bramble patch, Cassie. What else do you remember about it?'

She jerked around, suddenly startled by the tone of his voice, then her eyes seemed to clear as though some revelation dawned. 'Our hiding place.' Her voice tense, no more than whispering. Then she frowned, shook her head. 'But that was years ago.'

'Could be it's still there,' Maria Lucas suggested.

Mike was on his feet. There was only one way to find out.

'Think you can find it for me now?' he asked. Mike found it hard to keep the irritation and sarcasm from his voice. He was again fighting this strange double standard that had afflicted all his dealings with Cassie Maltham. On the one hand, he wanted to believe her, wanted to believe that the hypnosis had somehow revealed something deeply hidden in her subconscious. On the other hand . . . it had been too easy. One brief session and it was there? No. Somehow it didn't seem right. And, if this hidey hole of Cassie's had been as close as it sounded to Tan's hill, why the hell hadn't the searches revealed it? Why hadn't it appeared in Tynan's report?

He looked across at Dr Lucas and to his surprise saw that his doubts were echoed in her expression. She gestured with a little sideways nod of her head that they should talk outside.

Why hadn't the hidey hole shown up before?

He reached for the phone in the station office. Within minutes he'd arranged to meet Tynan at Tan's hill in an hour. He had to know the areas the original search had covered. What they had both missed.

Then he turned back to face Maria Lucas.

'She's lying to me.'

He expected denial; instead got a cool, thoughtful nod.

'It was too easy,' he went on. 'I've read about this

kind of thing. Sure, people bury things so deep the memory gets almost completely lost, but it can take session after session to get it in the clear again.'

He paused, offering his words as a challenge. Again, she nodded slowly.

'I'm not about to argue,' she said. 'I don't believe she'd put all the pieces together until now, but I do think she's been remembering bits of things ever since she got back here.'

'Like the dream woman?'

'Like the dream woman.' She paused as though uncertain of how to explain. 'You see, Mike, most of her life she's either been told she must forget all about Suzie, all about what happened and try to live life from now, or she's been in some way held to blame and not been allowed to forget it. That kind of double-bind . . . well, surely you can figure for yourself just what an effect it must have had.'

He frowned, not certain he wanted to imagine anything, furiously angry that Cassie Maltham might have been leading them all on some kind of wild-goose chase.

'Back then,' he demanded, 'you think she lied back then as well?'

Maria Lucas shook her head. 'No. Neither do I think she's been lying, not really lying, now. Sometimes Cassie finds it hard to sort out levels of actuality. What might seem like lies to an outsider may be her interpretation of the truth.'

Mike waved that away furiously. 'Lies are lies,' he

said. 'If she remembered about this place, remembered anything, then she should have told me. Think what that child and her family have been through. If something, *anything*, Cassie Maltham knew could have cut that by even an hour then she's guilty as hell in my book.'

He broke off, turned away, astounded at his own outburst. She came over to him, placed a careful, professional hand on his arm.

'I told you, Mike. I don't believe it all came together until now, not really. I think that, somehow, she almost needed permission to tell, needed the hypnosis as a way of losing responsibility for what she was about to tell you. Whatever else is going on in her head has been locked up for a very long time. You're going to have to be patient, have to understand that you won't get the whole story like some front-page tabloid confession. That's not the way the real world works.'

'Who do you think you're telling about the real world?' He snarled angrily. 'Try airing your theories to Suzie Ashmore's parents. To the Cassidys. To someone that's really lost a child. Try telling them they've got to be patient.'

'I thought I was,' she said softly.

He swung round, shocked and winded as though she'd struck him physically. 'How . . .' Then he remembered. Last night, he'd talked about Stevie, talked about Stevie alive, Stevie playing football for the first team, watching the Munsters at the local cinema. Stevie laughing at his stupid jokes. For a moment he felt betrayed. Anguished that she should use that against him, then he sighed. Allowed his shoulders to slump, lowered himself into the nearest chair.

'You're right,' he said. 'And I'm sorry.' He smiled. 'I'm beginning to know how Tynan felt. The Ashmore case dragged on for months. It got so that he was obsessed by it.'

'Well, you've got the child back this time.'

'And ended up with a murder enquiry instead.'

She almost laughed, he could see it. 'Well,' she said. 'No one ever said it was a perfect world.'

Chapter Sixteen

Tynan crouched beside Cassie, looking down the steepest slope of the hill and into the tangle of nettles and brambles that marked its foot. Mike had joined them, looking down, trying to glean from Cassie's broken explanations exactly where this hidey hole of hers was.

She'd been withdrawn and almost silent ever since they had left the station, and now they were on the hill she was only a little more communicative.

Down below them was a triangular formation where two fields intersected and the angle was too sharp to turn farm machinery easily. It had been left to grow wild, and, until the police search had cut it down, been a tangled thicket of briars, nettles and the dying remains of the summer's cow parsley.

Behind that was the hedge marking the field boundary and behind that, actually closest to them as they sat now, peering down over the side of the hill, was yet another thicket, backing onto the intersecting hedges of the two fields.

'You mean, actually somewhere in that lot?' Mike asked her.

Cassie nodded. 'It wasn't so thick then. We could get through. There was a place where the two hedges met that was much thicker. I suppose because no light could get through that bit and it was sort of hollow inside. Like a cave.'

Mike looked dubious. Then, maybe, but certainly not now. Surely the 'cave', even if it were still there, would be impossible to get to. Looking at it now, Mike could guess why this particular patch hadn't been thoroughly searched. From the field side it must look as if the thick May hedge backed straight against the hill. From Tan's hill itself the only way to see the thicket Cassie had pointed at was to lean out, lying almost flat on the ground, or, alternatively to go sliding down the hill itself and into the thorns and nettles. Tan's hill may not be big, in fact, as hills went it was downright insignificant, but the steep drop on this side was no less awkward for all that.

'If it is possible to get through,' Tynan was saying, 'then it would be possible for someone to get into the field by that gate at the far end, keep close to the hedge and maybe slip unnoticed through there and onto the hill.'

Mike shook his head. 'They'd need to be thorn-proof and the size of a weasel.'

He sighed heavily. He'd hoped too much, now he felt defeated by yet another dead end. 'We may as well take a look,' he said.

Tynan nodded. 'I'm going back to my car for the field glasses. I want to see the easiest way from the caravan.'

He pushed himself to his feet and set off down the other side. Mike got up.

'You going down there?' Maria Lucas asked him.

He nodded. 'Care to join me?'

'In these heels? No, thank you.'

He grinned at her, beckoned to the two constables he'd brought along and proceeded, slipping rather than walking, down the hillside. They followed, reluctantly, inelegant and undignified in blue serge and green wellingtons. There had been heavy rain the night before but, even so, the amount of mud seemed out of all proportion to what had been a heavy summer shower.

Mike cursed softly as he skidded sideways, gathered up a sticky handful of black mud as he put down a hand to steady himself. Something told him that climbing up was going to be even worse in shoes made for city walking and almost without grip.

What had Cassie been wearing on her feet?

He thought about it. That first time, when he'd found her searching so painfully for the woman in blue, she'd been barefoot. Her feet dirty and bruised enough for him to accept that she'd walked a fair distance that way. The last time, when she'd appeared from nowhere with Sara Jane and the woman's body ... He wasn't certain, but willing to bet she'd been wearing training shoes. He doubted it would have made either her descent or the climb back much easier and with a child wearing canvas lace-ups two sizes too big ... And what about a body?

Mud stains on the child's shorts, the report had mentioned that. On Cassie's jeans too, but then she'd been kneeling on the hill top and there had been a heavy dew.

He and the two constables had reached the bramble thicket now. They began to pull cautiously at it, seeing if it were possible to part the briar thicket. He remembered Cassie's description. She'd made it sound so easy. Confronted with the actuality, Mike figured he'd be as well off trying to part the Red Sea as push his way through this lot without thick gloves to protect his hands.

He cursed softly, angry at his own impatience and stupidity that made him come here so unequipped.

It seemed the two constables felt the same way. He heard one swear as the brambles scored more points against unprotected hands.

'We'd do better to wait, sir. Get some equipment down here.'

Mike nodded, inclined to agree with him but disinclined to give up without more of a fight. He felt so downright frustrated. Angry too that someone with his experience, someone who should have known better, should place such faith in flimsy possibilities. He glanced skyward. Grey clouds were gathering out to sea. He'd been here long enough to recognize the signs. Knew just how fast a seaborne storm could hit the coast even in summer. More rain and this place would be a quagmire. Glancing down he saw earth already churned up to an unacceptable degree. They should forget this for now. Come back better equipped when the storm had passed and the ground had had a chance to dry.

But stubbornly, he moved on, continued to pull and twist at the recalcitrant brambles, trying to ignore the pain as thorns caught and tore at his hand. He told himself that instinct led him to believe his answers lay somewhere on this hill, even though common sense dictated he was wasting everyone's time. He could just imagine Flint's reaction when he got to hear about this.

The first drops of rain had begun to fall, splashing heavily, adding to his sense of failure. Even the elements seemed to be telling him what a fool he was being.

He heard Tynan shouting from up above him and turned to see him waving the field glasses in the air, gesturing that they were heading back to the cars. Mike waved acknowledgement, then turned again to gaze in disgust at the seemingly insuperable barrier. Maybe in winter there would be a way through, when natural dieback would thin the tangle a little. Just now, the only way through as far as Mike could see was with a machete. He'd be willing to swear on oath that Cassie Maltham hadn't been carrying one of those either time he'd seen her on the hill.

'Sir? Should we call it a day, sir?' The young officer to his right was glancing up at the thickening, ink-swirled clouds and trying to remember that this was a senior officer.

Mike sighed heavily. 'May as well,' he said. 'There's nothing here.'

The young man smiled, evidently relieved. 'It was worth a look, sir,' he offered, his tone conciliatory.

Mike nodded. He poked one more time at the

thicket, scratching his hand again in the process, was about to tell the other constable to forget the whole thing when he was interrupted by an excited yell.

'Sir, you'd better take a look at this.'

The young constable was beaming, triumphant, holding aside in a thorn-scratched and bloodstained hand a mass of white-flowered brambles.

'Look, sir. Just lifted out like it was stuck together, sir. And, sir . . .' He was pointing excitedly like some enthusiastic game dog set for the kill. Mike was beside him, bending to peer into the narrow gap that had appeared once the officer had pulled the thick stems aside.

'God Almighty. She was right.' At that moment Mike would have given a month's pay for a flashlight. The darkening sky and the rain, falling now with increasing weight, blocked what little light would have filtered into this crazy passageway. He crouched, slid a little way inside peering into the gloom. He reached out a hand to touch the ground. Dry, bare soil, nothing much could grow where there was so little natural light. Cautiously, he moved further, realizing that he was no longer crouched beneath the bramble thicket but moving under the May hedge itself. Twigs and branches caught at his hair and the increasing gloom meant that he could see to go no further, but he'd seen enough. Cassie's 'hidey hole'. They'd been so close.

Had Sara been kept here all that time? No. Somehow that didn't seem likely, but she could have been brought back here, hidden for a brief period just before Cassie found her. Or was it Cassie who had brought her back here?

Caught somewhere between anger and exhilaration, Mike shook his head, shouted back to the two waiting for him.

'Call in. I want SOCO out here.'

'Now, sir? The rain . . .'

'I know. I know. See if you can rustle up tarps from somewhere. Local farmers are bound to have something. I want the whole area covered down, protect what we can.' He felt the ground again. He could hear the rain lashing at the foliage, feel the occasional drop leaking through where the natural . . . or not so natural . . . covering of brambles had been pulled aside, but had little doubt that, in spite of the storm, this area would remain protected. The main concern was to get the surrounding land covered, prevent the dip at the foot of the hill turning to bog. He wondered ruefully if he'd left it too late for that.

He was about to retreat, trying to turn and avoid the most vicious attacks from the hawthorn twigs when something caught his eye. It was only its alienness amongst the mass of green and brown that made him see it at all. Reaching up, Mike carefully drew the branch with its strange decoration down to eye level and, cautiously, so as not to detach it, fingered the scrap of blue ribbon that secured a long lock of soft blonde hair to the hawthorn branch.

'Sir.' The constable stuck a dripping head into Mike's enclosure. 'Sir, by the cars, sir, they say they've found something.'

'They say what?'

'No, sir, only that you'd better see it. Mr Tynan shouted from the top of the hill, sir.'

Somewhat reluctantly Mike scrambled out of his shelter and into the onslaught of the storm, full-fledged now and determined to blast the skin from his face with its surprising strength and coldness. A brief look told him that it was too late to worry about the tarpaulins. Water ran off the hill and into the channel at its foot. Carefully, he helped the constable to rearrange the brambles to cover the entrance, beckoned him to follow and began to struggle up the hill. The ground seemed to fall away from beneath their feet and fingers, as they dug deep for support.

They made it to the top, water running from their hair and clothes and hurried as fast as the wet land would allow them, off the hill and back along the Greenway.

This place seemed determined to keep its secrets, Mike thought, unreasonably angry. Just when they seemed to be getting somewhere it seemed that even the elements had turned against them.

They could see Tynan now, standing beside the patrol car that had brought the two young officers Mike had seconded. Rain dripped from Tynan's eyebrows, fairly poured from the end of his rather bulbous nose, but he appeared barely to notice. He was pointing instead at the back seat of the still locked car.

'Waited till you got here,' he said. 'There's something on the back seat wasn't there when we left.'

Mike signed to the officer to get the door unlocked,

threw it open and gazed in fascination at the pile of small, neatly stacked clothes on the back seat.

Mouth drying suddenly he asked in a voice that sounded choked and overtense, 'Sara Jane, the day she disappeared, the clothes she was wearing?' He remembered very well, but at that moment felt in need of confirmation, of someone to tell him he wasn't hallucinating.

'Red skirt, white blouse, socks with little frills at the top,' Tynan said softly.

'That's what I thought,' he said. 'That's just what I thought.' He stood back to let Tynan see, folded as neatly as if they'd just been packaged in a shop, the red, pleated skirt and white cotton blouse. On top, a pair of white pants decorated with tiny blue flowers and beside them white socks with a little frill of lace decorating their upper edge.

Chapter Seventeen

'Someone's out to make us look like a right load of Charlies.'

For once Flint was not seated at his desk but was pacing the room in a fit of agitation such as Mike had rarely seen.

'I'm being pressured to take you off the case, Mike, let the murder squad deal with it. It's only the fact it was your deal to begin with—'

'And that no one of importance had been murdered,' Mike put in, bitterly. 'Just some tramp that no one's going to miss.'

'Not true, Mike. Not true. I won't have talk like that.' He paused, stopped his pacing and said solemnly, 'I'm beginning to like your attitude less and less DI Croft and, let me tell you, the pressure's on for us to get answers.'

Mike waved an exasperated hand at his superior. He didn't like the way things were going any more than Flint did, but if the man thought he could do better . . .

He switched off, aware that Flint was still mid rant but that little of any importance was likely to be said. Instead, he slumped back in his seat and stared hard at the plastic laminate pretending to be wood that faced Flint's desk, examining in minute detail the precise pattern of artificial wood grain.

It was still raining. Looked set to last the night and, Mike knew, it would take a good morning of hot sun before he could let anyone down to look at what they'd found.

He was aware, dimly, that Flint's tone had changed. Mike realized that his period of indulgent pontification was over and that he should give him at least a modicum of attention once more.

Flint was asking what he planned to do next.

'Depends on the weather,' Mike told him. 'Meantime, we've sent the kid's clothes to forensics. When they've done we'll get the Cassidys to make a positive I.D. I've not much doubt though, that they're Sara Jane's.'

'This shrink any help?' Flint asked abruptly. It took Mike a second or two to realize he meant Dr Lucas.

'Matter of fact she's been very co-operative,' Mike told him. Flint looked suspicious.

'Just remember, Mike, this is business. I don't interfere with what my people do off duty, but she's part of an investigation.'

Mike looked coldly at him. So news of his dinner with Maria Lucas had reached Flint? There was a saying that within the station a flea couldn't fart without everyone getting wind of it.

'It's Doctor Lucas's patient that's part of the investigation,' he said quietly. 'Not Doctor Lucas.'

Flint snorted. 'Come off it, Mike. Doctor–patient relationships and all that. If you think this Lucas woman won't protect her own and Mrs Maltham's interests, you're far more of a fool than I've been led to believe.'

Saturday morning was bright. Clear skies and hot sunshine from early in the day. Perhaps, Mike thought, the storm gods felt they'd persecuted him enough and were willing now to give him an even break.

With luck, by noon, the ground would have dried enough for SOCO to make another attempt at the site.

He drove out to Tan's hill as soon as he thought there would be a chance that the teams, set to be there from nine, would have had the opportunity to do something, and arrived just after eleven. He stood for some time at the top of the hill, watching the forensic teams do their work. The team leader had glanced up and nodded acknowledgement at him a few moments before, but he didn't go down. Mike was realistic, experienced enough to know that at this stage he could only be in the way.

Instead, he watched, feeling as always the strange sense of unreality as these meticulous assessors of the breakdowns in other people's lives went about their business, photographing, grid marking, carefully cutting back the outer layers of foliage after recording the position and characteristics of each one.

Mike had once had the opportunity to watch archaeologists at work. This was very like that time. The slow, unhurried attention both groups gave to their work. Their seeming isolation from the schedules and concerns of the rest of the world. Mike sighed, feeling a little impatient, spread his raincoat on the ground – he'd come slightly more prepared this time – and sat down to drink flask coffee and wait for something to happen.

It was more than three hours before it did.

Three hours of watching them dismantle the bramble patch piece by piece. Three hours of photographs, of pegged references marked out on the increasingly exposed ground. Of soil samples taken where slightly discoloured patches were disturbed.

They found his scrap of ribbon hanging with its pathetic little tail of blonde hair and he watched as it was photographed in situ, then snipped, complete with the twig it was attached to, bagged up ready for testing.

The entire briar patch had been removed now and Mike could just glimpse the entrance to the hidey hole. He moved himself further down the hill, perched somewhat precariously about half-way down and watched in fascination as a female member of the team crawled into the space now revealed. Like a green cave, Cassie had said, and she was right. It was – though Mike was confounded as to how – twenty years on, and it was still there.

He ducked his head down in an attempt to peer inside. He could see the woman, a dim outline on hands and knees, but it was difficult to make out

206

details. Even exposed as it now was, the gap beneath the hedge was still a twilit area, a place of shadows and naked earth. Perhaps it was not so surprising that it had been so well preserved. No light meant nothing was growing, and the natural outward curve that the main branches of the hawthorn made around the womb-like gap had prevented a natural filling in by its own offshoots.

'Pure fluke,' Mike said aloud. Then wondered. Could someone else have been aware of this place? Kept it clear? Perhaps the woman whose body they'd found on the hill, or others like her who'd welcome any shelter.

He could see the woman scraping soil samples now, using a grid to mark where each came from, reminding him again of the archaeological dig he had seen.

She passed them out to one of her companions, taking from him in return something that looked like a wire probe. Carefully, she began to push the instrument into the ground. One area seemed to have attracted her particularly. She took more samples, then, taking something else – it looked like a bent spoon to Mike – began to remove a little more of the top soil from that point.

Mike edged closer. It was clear from the sudden tension and the way that work had ceased all around her that the woman had found something. With the delicate precision of a surgeon the woman excised her find from the hard-crusted, loose earth. A tiny bone.

At first Mike sat down again and began to relax.

Some small animal had died in there, he figured. The woman had marked her find and retreated from the hole, placing her find carefully in a marked bag.

Mike moved excitedly as the team leader beckoned to him.

'It's a bone from a finger,' he said. 'A child's finger. My guess is we have a body down there.'

Chapter Eighteen

The news of the child's skeleton screamed at Mike from the morning headlines. He threw the papers aside after only the briefest of glances and slumped back in his chair feeling thoroughly deflated. After spending most of the previous day observing the careful excavation, seeing to the reports and becoming more cognizant with the post-mortem of the woman they'd found on the hill he'd returned to the station to find that he no longer headed the investigation.

'The child's been found,' Flint told him. 'We've been told to hand over to the experts.' His tone had been wry, disapproving, but accepting.

Mike had argued for a full hour, but to no effect. The fact was the directive had come from higher up than Flint and the most he could do was to approve Croft's secondment to the murder enquiry.

'They're keen to have you, Mike, I've been told to make that very clear.' Mike had looked askance at him. 'It's a policy decision. Best use of available manpower.'

Mike stared angrily at the office wall. He'd not realized just how strong his personal involvement in this had become. How much he considered it *his* investigation.

'The other thing, Mike, is that they want to play down the more . . . esoteric elements of the case. It doesn't look good, you know, for us to seem like we're chasing ghosts.'

Mike had laughed aloud at that, at the irony of it. 'But that's just what we damn well have been doing, isn't it, sir?' He continued to laugh softly as if at a private joke.

Flint gave him an anxious look. 'Mike,' he said quietly, 'maybe you're pushing yourself too hard on this one, getting too involved.' He paused, then said almost gently, 'You've leave due to you, why don't you take it? Get yourself out of this for a while.'

Mike turned sharply to look at him. 'That official policy, too, is it?'

Flint shook his head. 'No, Mike, my personal recommendation. No one says you have to take it . . .' He left the unsaid 'but' in the air between them and went on, 'I think you're too involved. Too close.' He paused again, then added almost casually, 'Tynan got too involved you know. He had a good future ahead of him, but the Ashmore case finished all that. He couldn't let go of it, continued the investigation in his own time even after it had officially been shelved. His ideas became, well, let's just say a little strange.' He looked meaningfully at Mike, who said nothing, just returned his gaze to the cracked and peeling paintwork of the office wall.

'It would be a waste for the same thing to happen to you. Take a break.'

Mike had continued to stare for a few moments longer, the paintwork with its network of cracks and discoloured patches left by decaying sticky tape suddenly deeply absorbing. Then he shook his head. 'I'm not John Tynan, sir,' he said. 'Though I've learnt to respect his reasons.' He hesitated. 'It's hard to let go when there's a kid involved.'

Flint nodded. 'Sure it is, Mike, but there's still such a thing as objectivity.' He frowned then added in a more conciliatory tone. 'Look, the team's being assembled, pulled together from all over the division. The first major briefing won't be until Monday.'

'Monday?' Mike was surprised. Generally murder investigations were a little faster off the mark.

Flint shrugged. 'Earliest reports indicate the child's body has been in the ground for quite a time. We're still running preliminary checks on the woman, trying to get an I.D. on her, there's not much to be done here. If you won't take leave then you'll at least take your Sunday.'

So here he was. Sunday morning, a free day ahead of him to use as he liked and already bored to tears.

The telephone, piercing and insistent, broke through his thoughts. It was Bill Enfield. Mike felt his spirits lift a little.

'Good morning to you. Enjoying your break, you jammy bugger?'

'Hey, that should be you jammy bugger, *sir.*'

'Sorry, officers on off days don't count,' Bill told him.

Mike laughed. 'So what can I do for you?' he asked.

'You can accept Rose's invitation to lunch.'

'You're not working?'

'I don't live at the office, not quite. No, I've been seconded to this team of experts we've got coming in, same as you, they don't need the likes of me till morning. Not that I'm grumbling mind, my last three Sundays off I've ended up going in so I'm enjoying it while I can.'

'Well, are you sure you want me intruding?'

'Don't talk so bloody wet, Mike. Rose wants to meet you and John's already on his way. We eat at one-thirty.'

Mike heard the phone click as Bill broke the connection, smiled to himself. Well, it was far better than spending a Sunday alone and if John Tynan was going to be there . . . Briefly, he reminded himself that he was meant to be resting, forgetting all about the Ashmore case, and Cassie Maltham and the unknown woman, and the child they had found. He stopped thinking about it for the ten minutes it took him to shave, an activity he'd never quite managed to share with other concerns, and then forgot all about forgetting, let his imagination have full rein as he drove the few miles to Bill Enfield's house.

Tynan's car was already there and through an open window Mike could hear him laughing at something. He heard too a woman's voice, catch the slow, soft burr of the local accent as she spoke.

It was Rose who answered his knock at the door, Bill following her close behind, making the introduction.

'I'm so pleased to meet you,' she told him. 'Bill says you're a big improvement on that last one. Now come on in.'

Her directness surprised him, he caught Bill's look over his wife's shoulder and laughed. 'Thank you,' he said, 'and thank you as well for the invitation. It's very kind.'

'Not a bit of it,' Rose said, smiling broadly at him. 'It's nice to have company. Don't get enough of it these days, what with the family grown up and moved away. Now go and make yourself comfortable.'

Mike watched her as she marched back into the kitchen, then looked back at Bill. Like enough to be book-ends, he thought. Rose didn't have quite Bill's roundness, but she certainly seemed to share his temperament. He grinned contentedly and allowed himself to be ushered into the sitting room.

John was already well ensconced, surrounded by the Sunday papers.

'We've made it to the front page two weeks in a row,' he said, reaching over and dumping the whole pile into Mike's lap.

'I know,' he replied. 'I saw some of them earlier on.'

'We've been told to handle this one carefully. Play down the weird bits,' Bill added. 'Though how in the world we're meant to do that, God alone knows.'

'Any word on the skeleton?' Mike asked.

Bill shook his head. 'Read the papers and you'll have about all I've been told. Seems the age, estimated height and the like are the same as the Ashmore girl, but the dental records don't match. No, this is another one.'

'Another?' Mike was startled, he'd been certain that the bones had to be Suzie Ashmore. The thought that there might be another body hadn't crossed his mind.

'There's a lot of speculation that the bones've been in the ground more than twenty years too. First thing tomorrow we start sifting missing-persons reports from before the Ashmore case.'

Mike shook his head in disbelief. 'And they said our connection was tenuous.'

'We might be getting ourselves a geriatric murderer at this rate,' Bill commented. 'Or, of course, there may be no connection at all. Murders do happen independently,' he added.

'Yes,' Mike said, 'of course they do. Maybe Flint's right, I've been looking at this thing so closely I can't see the wood for the proverbial trees.'

Tynan laughed. 'In this case it should be the proverbial hawthorn bushes. How are the hands?'

Mike glanced down. 'Sore,' he said.

'You got off lightly. Bill was telling me the two constables helping you on Friday had to get themselves tetanus jabs.'

Bill nodded confirmation. 'We've got the pair of them walking round with bruised backsides,' he said.

Mike laughed, then asked, 'So do we know who's heading this thing then? Flint wasn't able to tell me.'

214

'Far as I know it hasn't been confirmed yet. Be either Cunningham or Peters.' He grinned knowingly at Mike. 'Either way you'll be all right, Mike, there's neither one of them likes scrambling about in the mud. Desk junkies the pair of them.'

Mike said nothing, accepting Bill's assessment. He had, after all, been around long enough to know; it was Mike that was the new kid.

Tynan was bending to scrabble for something beside his chair. He straightened, producing a stack of files and cuttings' books already familiar to the others.

'Bill told me on the phone,' he said, 'about this body maybe not being Suzie's. It got me thinking.' He rummaged in one of the files, withdrew a sheaf of notes and some scraps of paper. 'Man called Emsbury was vicar then. He's retired now but I've checked, he's still living in the area. Well, at the time Suzie Ashmore went missing I got to know him quite well.' He shuffled the notes further, sifted out what he wanted and handed them to Mike. 'Emsbury was a stranger round here, in other words he'd only been around for the best part of a decade.' He grinned at Mike. 'He was something of a local history buff, liked the local legends and so on.'

'Plenty of those,' Bill commented.

'Certainly are,' Tynan confirmed. 'Most relevant to us, though, is something that happened about twenty years before Emsbury came here. There was a child. Little girl called Emma Cooper, eleven years old, disappeared without trace. I'll let you guess where from.' He paused, looked thoughtfully at Mike who

215

was reading his way through Tynan's cramped, hand-written notes. 'I'd dismissed it as coincidence really. This little Cooper girl, rumours have it she was un-happy at home, father hit the bottle then hit the kids, you know the scenario, so when she went everyone just thought she'd run away.'

Mike looked thoughtful. 'Worth looking into if the date's right,' he said, 'but it was fifty years ago, going to be very hard to prove.' He looked again at the notes, then at the photocopies Tynan had taken of period news reports, comparing them to the Ashmore case and the disappearance of Sara Jane Cassidy. Two children, the reports said, Emma and a friend, a child of the same age, playing on the Greenway. Emma had run on ahead after the dog, her friend said she'd seen Emma turn the corner around Tan's hill, had begun to run after her then she'd slipped and fallen down. When she got up again and went after her friend she couldn't be found.

'It doesn't say,' Mike commented, 'whether there was a time lapse between the child falling over and her going after her friend again.'

'No,' John agreed, 'it doesn't, but it makes you wonder.'

'I remember it,' Bill said unexpectedly. 'I was only a kid at the time, but I remember it happening. They arrested the father, didn't they?'

Tynan nodded. 'Yes, but the body was never found and there was no real proof. He'd been heard to threaten the child and everyone knew he had a violent temper, but then he'd apparently been heard to threaten just about anyone who got in his way when he'd been drinking.' He shrugged. 'The case was never closed, just shelved, like the Ashmore affair.'

Mike laughed shortly. 'I can see the delight on Flint's face if we tell him we want to re-open an unsolved fifty-year-old case,' he said.

'Well, one thing's for sure,' Bill added. 'Cassie Maltham wasn't even born then. No link that way at least.'

'Well, that's something to be glad about,' Tynan affirmed. 'I take it you're still looking to connect her with Sara Jane?'

Mike shook his head. 'I really can't say. It's possible. What does seem likely is that she knew, subconsciously at least, that the child could be there. And this woman, the one from her dream, how she ties in to all this . . .'

'There was an itinerant seen close to where the children were playing when Suzie was lost,' Tynan reminded him.

Mike nodded. 'Yes, but does it seem possible it would be the same one? That was twenty years ago. Our mystery woman would be maybe in her late-twenties, early-thirties at most. Would Cassie, even if she saw the woman then, even if it was the same woman, would she be able to make up the twenty years difference and recognize her as such?'

'Who knows?' Tynan waved a dismissive hand. 'The mind is capable of some strange things. Someone figured out once that we recognize faces by referring to only about a half-dozen factors. Maybe if they stay consistent it's possible to fill in the gaps.'

Mike thought about it, then shook his head. 'No. That's pushing coincidence too far even for this mess. We've got to start dealing with facts.'

They were interrupted by Rose, bringing coffee in a large blue pot. She set it down on the table and busied herself pouring, telling them that dinner would be about another half-hour. Mike smiled his thanks, wondered, as she sat down with them, if they ought to turn the conversation elsewhere. Bill had no such qualms.

'Been talking about the Cooper girl,' he said. 'You remember, the little lass that disappeared when we were both kids.'

Rose frowned in concentration for a moment, then her expression cleared and she nodded. 'Certainly, I remember, be about ten or eleven she would be. Think that could be who you've found, Mike?'

Mike replied that he didn't know, that it was possible. Rose frowned again then went on, 'Hell of a noise was made at the time, but they never did find her.' She shook her head sadly. 'My mum, she wouldn't let any of us out of the house for weeks after that. She was superstitious like.' She nudged her husband cheerfully as though reminding him of a joke. 'Said they'd no right to let children play on the fairy hill anyhow.' She turned to Mike. 'You know what they used to say about the place, load of rubbish that was, used to say it was a gateway. A road into fairyland, if you please.'

She got up to offer more coffee. Mike commented, 'It seems that was a popular idea even up to Suzie Ashmore's time.'

Rose nodded. 'Some things are slow to change,' she said. 'We might have television, satellites, news in minutes from all across the world, but some things just cling on.' She paused as though searching for the right analogy. 'Like thistles,' she said.

'Thistles?' Mike was momentarily mystified.

'Thistles,' she repeated calmly. 'Long roots, you know. Try and pull them up without gloves on and you know about it. Deep tap roots too and you only have to leave the smallest piece in the ground and there you'll be, having to uproot it all over again.'

Mike nodded. He wouldn't like to comment on the botanical accuracy of the statement, but he knew what she meant. Odd ideas and misconceptions had become the heartwood of this affair. Maybe it needed a different approach. Maybe they'd been looking so hard to make connections that they'd forgotten how to see straight. He took a deep breath.

'Supposing,' he said slowly, 'that there is no connection. Supposing that Cassie Maltham being here is pure coincidence and we should treat this as a whole new series.'

They were looking at him, all three of them, as though he'd suddenly lost his mind. Mike exhaled, a deep, exasperated sigh. 'No,' he said, 'I don't believe that either, but I'm damned if I can fathom it.'

He glanced down again at the cuttings and notes

Tynan had given him. 'You say this vicar, Emsbury, he's still living around here?'

Tynan nodded. 'Yes, we've kept in vague contact. Christmas cards, that sort of thing.'

'Go and see him, see if there's a thread, not just to the Cooper girl but to any others.'

Tynan looked askance at him.

Mike shook his head. 'I don't know what I'm looking for, John, probably nothing, but it seems to me we've got three cases which may, or may not be connected. It's worth a look.'

'Wouldn't police records be better?' Tynan asked.

Mike grimaced. 'No. Not really. For one thing we've been told to play down the weirdness, as Bill says. For another thing, what I'm looking for might go back further.'

'Oh?'

Mike almost looked embarrassed. He said, 'The truth is, John, I'm probably flying off at a tangent and sending you on a wild-goose chase. It seems to me, though, that a place like the Greenway and Tan's hill, with the kind of reputation it's got, well, maybe there's a reason for it.' He hesitated, then added, 'Like Rose's thistle. The original plant is long gone but this one's had time to set seeds.'

Rose looked at him in surprise. 'You surely don't believe in all that witch and fairy nonsense,' she demanded.

Mike laughed shortly. 'No, but what I believe doesn't matter. It's what other people believe about the place that does. Maybe their ideas about it trigger something very deep, something inside them that's normally hidden, kept in check.' He shrugged again. 'I'm probably way off base,' he said, 'but anything's worth a look.'

Mike could feel that John looked speculatively at him, but made no comment. The fact was, though he was far too embarrassed ever to admit it, the dream he'd had a couple of nights before, continued to haunt him. It had disturbed him enough for him to have spent the last few nights sleeping with the light on, and to have made his visits to Tan's hill episodes equipped with a slight frisson of unease, even in daylight. He had to admit to himself that nothing would entice him there at night. Stupid, he knew, particularly as all three children had gone missing in the full light of day, but it was a notion that he couldn't shake. Perhaps, like Cassie Maltham, he was going to have to learn to lay his ghosts when this was over. The thought filled him with unease and vague, but potent, self-contempt.

He had not left the Enfields' until evening. The talk had moved on to other things and Mike had found himself looking at albums, listening to reminiscences. He'd been quite content to do so though, not realizing before just how starved he had felt of casual, easy company, of a sense of family. He arrived back at the flat feeling more relaxed, but also, even more acutely aware of its functional emptiness. He'd rented the place partly furnished, and not without difficulty, accommodation, other than the holiday type, being in short supply. He had added what was required for his immediate needs and left it at that. Looking around now at the two armchairs, the TV, the few bits and pieces of assorted and very utilitarian furnishing he'd bothered to purchase, the tiny flat had an air of transience, of dissatisfaction.

He felt the ebullient mood of earlier evening dissolving, decided to check his messages, and perhaps go for a walk, even phone the hotel to see if Dr Lucas had returned yet. The idea cheered him somewhat. She'd told him she had to return home but would be back on Sunday. She might well be back already.

He wandered somewhat listlessly over to the answerphone, pressed playback. The first message was from his ex-wife, reminding him that the house sale was about to go through and there were things he had to sign. She sounded cheerful, businesslike, quite unlike the woman he'd been married to. The second message made him turn, gaze intently at the answerphone. 'Sergeant Holmwood here, sir. Sorry to disturb your Sunday but a Doctor Lucas wanted you to get in touch with her.' Mike cursed inwardly that he'd not thought to give Maria his home number. It hadn't seemed worth it, he was hardly ever there. 'It seems Mrs Maltham's been taken ill, sir. She wants you to call her asap on the following number.'

Mike grabbed a pen, began to scribble down the number, suddenly angry with himself for not being available.

He checked that was the end of the message and pounced on the telephone, rapping impatiently with the pen as he listened to the dialling tone.

'Come on, come on . . . Yes. I want to speak to Doctor Maria Lucas. Tell her it's Mike Croft, that I've only just got her message.'

'Would you hold please, Mr Croft? I'll have her paged.'

Mike held, impatiently, his ears offended by the tinny sound of 'soothing' music being played to him. It seemed like a long time before he heard the familiar, pleasing voice of Maria Lucas replacing the Muzak. He apologized profusely for not getting back to her sooner. Launched himself into an explanation, which, characteristically, she cut short.

'Mike, behave yourself and listen.'

Grinning to himself, Mike proceeded to do as he was told.

'Cassie's here, back at Oaklands, with me.' Oaklands, he remembered was the psychiatric hospital where Cassie Maltham had been treated before.

'On a section?'

'No, that wasn't necessary. She's here voluntarily and will be undergoing assessment tomorrow, but I don't think a section will prove relevant. Fact is, Mike, she's running scared and this is as safe a place as she can get.'

'Is Fergus with you?'

'Yes. He's gone home for tonight. The Thomases are still at the caravan, but they're going to have to get back to their jobs soon, so unless you need them . . .

223

Look, Mike, I'm bushed. I'll see you in the morning, no, I'll meet you for lunch. The best thing you can do meantime is to talk to the Thomases, they were with Cassie, be able to fill in the details, and I'll be able to tell you more tomorrow.'

She sounded uncharacteristically cagey, but it was clear he was going to have to be satisfied. He said goodbye to her and glanced at his watch. Not quite eight-fifteen. It would take about forty minutes to get out to the caravan. Mike turned, headed out and back to his car. Sod the rest day. Running scared, Maria had said. Scared of what? He felt suddenly angry with himself for not pressing her for answers over the phone. Common sense told him that he wouldn't have got any.

Sighing impatiently, he concentrated on making the best speed he could along the winding roads.

Anna turned weary eyes on him, then she went back to staring down into her cup. Slowly revolving it on the saucer, swirling the dregs of cold liquid round and round like some fortune-teller about to predict a bleak future.

'It was just awful,' she said. 'I'd never seen her like that. When she was ill before, I didn't really see her much.' She broke off, swallowed, painfully. 'Poor Cassie.' She looked up again at Mike, a swift, appealing glance, as though trying to make him understand. 'She just kept saying these things, about the woman on the hill, you know, the dead one.'

224

'Saying things like what?' Mike asked gently.

Anna looked embarrassed, glanced over at Simon, who answered reluctantly, as though he felt it a betrayal of friendship.

'She kept saying that it was Suzie. The woman, I mean. We kept telling her that it couldn't be, that the dead woman was too old for one thing, but she wouldn't have it.'

He glanced at Anna as though for confirmation and she nodded anxiously. 'She got really upset, really angry, so Fergus went down to the village to phone Doctor Lucas. By the time she'd got here, Cassie was saying different things altogether.' She hesitated, as though not certain how to explain what had happened to her friend. 'It was like she was trying to work something out. Get it straight in her head and didn't quite know where to start.' She broke off and looked over at Simon once more.

Mike prompted them. 'So then, what did she say next?'

Anna turned and looked at him as though coming to a sudden decision. Her eyes showing the bewilderment she felt, she said, 'Cassie started saying that she'd killed her. That she'd found a big stick and hit her over and over again until she didn't move any more. She kept lifting her arms above her head like this.' She raised her own arms in demonstration. 'Then bringing them down, like this.' Anna shook her head slowly. 'I don't believe Cassie could have done that.' She turned to look directly at Mike once more. 'Cassie's not danger-

225

ous. She's been hurt, she's tried to hurt herself, but she's not dangerous.'

She was looking for reassurance, but Mike felt he could make no comment. He knew how common it was for the disturbed to take on guilt that wasn't their own. In this case, though, was it possible? Common sense argued that Cassie had opportunity. Her elusive morning walks alone would give her that and the motive could be one in her head that needed no external reasoning to make it adequate.

Simon had reached for his wife's hand. 'She didn't stick to that for long, though. Like Anna said, it was as though she was trying to work things out, as though the memories had got all jumbled. She knew there was something she had to remember about the woman dying and about Suzie, but she just couldn't get it into perspective.'

'So the story changed,' Mike asked, realizing, as Simon frowned, that he could have made a better choice of words.

'Yes,' Simon said, somewhat coldly. 'She kept insisting that Suzie was dead. It was like something in her head had cleared then. As though she'd finally straightened things out. She kept saying that the woman had killed her.'

'The woman whose body we found?' Mike asked quickly.

Simon looked puzzled for a moment, then said, 'I think so. It was getting very confusing by then.'

'Did she say how her cousin died?'

Simon looked at him in surprise. 'You're taking this seriously then?' he asked.

Mike thought for a moment before replying, then spoke cautiously. 'I think it has to be taken note of, at the very least. The dream woman turned out to be real, though Cassie's images of her were just as confused. Maybe something of this will help us.'

'I can't believe Cassie did anything wrong,' Anna protested. 'Cassie's just not like that,' she finished, sounding a little helpless, evidently not knowing what to think any more. She got up, took the cups to the sink. 'I'll make more tea,' she said, speaking to no one in particular.

Simon was silent, thinking about what to say next. Mike watched Anna as she filled the kettle, set it to heat on the Calor stove. It was, he noted, a whistling kettle, like Tynan's. Did Anna race the kettle, he wondered vaguely? No, he decided, that wasn't her style.

He glanced around, not wanting to break the profound silence. The noise of the gas flame the only active sound in the entire room. Simon sat, head bent, glaring at the tabletop and Anna stood beside the tiny sink, arms folded in front of her, a look of puzzlement creasing her face, her neat, well-cut hair, for once not quite so tidy, and her make-up looking as though she'd not renewed it since morning.

At last he spoke. 'Cassie claims now that her cousin died way back then. Yes?'

Simon nodded.

'Which implies she must have witnessed her murder?'

Again, Simon nodded.

'So, the body. Did she say where the body was?'

Simon hesitated this time, looked to Anna for support. 'Not exactly,' he said. 'But from the way she was talking it was where you found the skeleton.'

Mike nodded slowly. Well, the hidey hole could be searched again. No problems there.

'There was something else really strange,' Simon went on. 'Right from when we heard about the body she kept saying that it wasn't Suzie.'

'She knew that?'

Simon nodded. 'Absolutely adamant,' he said.

Mike thought carefully. Cassie and her cousin had played often on the Greenway, knew the hidey hole, played there. What if they'd found the skeleton all that time ago? It hadn't been buried deep, the experts said the grave was no more than a hurriedly made scrape in the ground. It didn't seem right somehow. Surely, finding something like that when you are ten or twelve years old would be terrifying? Something to run home to safety from and cry to your mother about?

Or would it? Children have a strange sense of honour, of logic. What if they were more afraid of something else? Or what if Cassie hadn't realized just what the bones were until the skeleton had been unearthed? No, surely that didn't make sense. Even if she'd not known as a child that these were human remains, wouldn't she have realized as she grew older and thought to tell someone about their childhood find?

He shook his head again. No, the last thing Cassie Maltham had wanted was anything that could make it necessary for her to come back here. If Dr Lucas's experiments were to be believed, Cassie had blocked all memory of the hidey hole from her mind until now.

So. What then?

Anna had returned to the table and was pouring the tea. 'We talked it over,' she said, 'after Cassie and Fergus had gone. We think she did see something, maybe even Suzie being killed, that scared her so much she had to forget about it.'

Simon nodded. 'We think they must have known about the skeleton too. I mean, they played there. Maybe they found it.'

Mike sipped his tea in silence. Something at the back of his mind told him that, finally, he was on the right lines. That in some way, Suzanne Ashmore's death (if she was dead, he reminded himself, he had that one to prove yet) was linked to the children's knowledge of the skeleton. Had someone found out that they knew? Frightened them into silence then tried to make certain by killing Suzie?

Then why spare Cassie's life?

He reminded himself abruptly that this was the Ashmore case he was discussing with himself. That he then had to take account of the Cassidy abduction and the woman whose body they'd found on the hill.

Where was the link? Was Sara Jane telling the truth about remembering nothing?

And the woman – her injuries had been horrifying and had the look of deliberate and premeditated infliction. How did that fit in?

Mike finished his tea, suddenly aware that the Thomases were watching him closely. He rose to go.

'I'm meeting Doctor Lucas tomorrow,' he said. 'Perhaps we'll all know more by then.' He paused, looking at Simon and Anna, strain showing on their faces, reminding him of just how tired he was himself.

'Meantime,' he said, 'try and get some sleep.'

Simon laughed, a sharp uneasy sound. 'Just try,' Mike said and left them, still sitting at the table staring miserably into cups of cold tea.

Outside the wind had risen, the rather wan half-moon illuminated the feathered edges of rapidly scudding clouds. Glancing out over the headland Mike could glimpse the sea, denser black against the darkness of the night sky. It was well after ten, but even so, dark early for the time of year. There should still be some evening grey in the clouds, perhaps even a touch of red close to the horizon. He shrugged. No one seemed to have informed the night that it had come a little too early.

Chapter Nineteen

The drive out to Embury's had given John Tynan plenty of time for thought and to consider if he really was chasing wild geese. He was growing increasingly worried about Mike, liked the man, thought him a good policeman and was concerned that the investigation seemed to be taking hold of him in much the same way the Ashmore case had caught Tynan himself.

Prior to Suzie Ashmore's disappearance, he'd been tipped for promotion, been the divisional go-getter. After – he was lucky not to have ended up on permanent traffic duty. He felt real reluctance to maybe seeing Mike go the same way, especially as, in this case, the child had been found safe.

There was an autumnal tang already in the air, unseasonably early though it might be. Tynan drove with the windows wide open, enjoying the feeling of being just that fraction too cold for comfort. It would, he knew, in the long run simply add to the pleasure of warm sunlight on his arms and back when he got out of the car.

Embury's place was somewhat off the beaten track; or rather, Tynan thought wryly, that was exactly where it was. It had been a tied cottage not so long ago, and was reachable only by driving along a gated, rut-ridden pretence at a trackway. He could feel his car, like himself, a little past its sell-by date, groaning and complaining as its elderly and inadequate suspension strove to cope with the bumps and grooves carved by the passage of tractors.

He could feel his own suspension pleading for reprieve also, was glad when Embury's tiny cottage came into view.

Embury must have heard the car, was waiting for him on the doorstep. He'd changed little, Tynan reflected. Hair somewhat greyer, perhaps even slightly more sparse on top and an odd wrinkle or two added around the eyes. He stepped forward as John eased himself out of the car, extending a long-fingered bony hand towards him.

'John! This is a pleasant thing. When I got your call I couldn't quite believe it.'

Embury seemed so genuinely pleased to receive him that Tynan felt a momentary guilt at having not come out here before.

He took the extended hand. 'You're right out of the way here.'

Embury nodded. 'Literally in the middle of nowhere,' he responded, though it was said cheerfully enough.

'You live here alone?'

'No. No as a matter of fact I don't. I have this rather good arrangement with the farmer who owns this place. I let a couple of the unmarried workers share the biggest room and he keeps my rent down to almost nothing. Truth is, I hardly see them except at meal times. My rooms are at the back and very self-contained so it works out very well.'

He leaned confidentially towards Tynan. 'I think they get a little uptight about bringing their lady friends back, you know, having to share the house with an ex-vicar, but I do try to keep out of their way. Cough loudly before I come into the kitchen and that sort of thing.'

His eyes were laughing as Tynan turned to glance at him. He'd forgotten much about Embury but the laughter that was never far from the pale blue eyes was something he remembered very distinctly.

'It's still a bit out of the way though, isn't it?' He had paused, was looking back over the expanse of stubble waiting to be ploughed back. The road he had come in on was, he estimated, about a half mile away. A half mile that would be practically impassable in winter.

They turned now towards the cottage – a dour Victorian brick affair. Solid and utilitarian, not really pretty enough and a little too isolated to attract the tourist market.

Embury made tea and they exchanged polite comments, Tynan pacing the length of the kitchen, gazing first out of one window then the next, then following Embury through to the small room at the back he'd turned into his study.

'Sit down, sit down,' he said. 'If you can't find space then just put things on the floor.'

Tynan gingerly moved a pile of books from one of

the armchairs and placed them as neatly as he could beside the chair. It looked, from the state of the room, that years' worth of visitors had been taking Embury's advice and stacking things in any available space. Embury excavated a place to sit down, poured the tea which he'd set on a rather precarious looking table between them and then looked invitingly at Tynan.

'Well, then,' he said, 'and what can I do for you?'

Tynan smiled. Directness had always been one of Embury's traits. He returned with equal measure. 'You can tell me about the Cooper family. Young Emma that disappeared and that father of hers. What happened to them?'

Embury smiled. 'Ah,' he said. 'The other Greenway mystery. Seems to attract them somehow, doesn't it?' He paused for a moment as though considering. 'Some places are like that, you know. It's as though they call the tragic to them. Almost magnetic in some cases.' He paused, took a sip of tea. Tynan wondered whether he should prompt him, remembering very well how Embury could become side-tracked and run along quite happily at a complete tangent without ever noticing that he'd changed subjects.

This time he didn't though. The pale eyes twinkled again. 'But you don't want my theories on that,' he said. 'The Coopers. Yes, sad case.' He paused speculatively again. 'The news reports say you've found a body.'

'Not me,' Tynan reminded him. 'But, yes, the

remains of a child, been in the ground for quite some time.'

'Not the Ashmore girl then.'

'It doesn't seem likely, but it might be Emma Cooper.' He looked somewhat apologetic. 'There's not a lot I can tell you, I'm afraid. Officially, I've no part in this, but I've been tagging along.'

'And being very useful too, I've no doubt.'

'Er, the Coopers?' Tynan prompted as Embury seemed to be gathering himself for some alternative tirade.

'Oh, yes. Now where was I?' Embury settled himself back in his chair and began.

'William Cooper was a drunkard. Oh, but then you probably know that. But for all that he drank I'm told he was a good stockman, gentle and efficient round anything that had four legs.' He laughed, a little sadly. 'Shame of it was, he was no good around anything with less. Treated his family as though they were nothing more than chattels. Always wanted a son, you see, and his wife gave him two daughters. Not that there's any excuse there, of course.'

'What happened to her? The wife I mean.'

'Oh, she died not long after the second one was born. Probably something very avoidable, but you know how it was.'

Tynan nodded sympathetically.

'Well, for a long time the grandmother, one side or another, his I think, she took care of the little ones, but when the youngest was about five or six he came to get

235

JANE ADAMS

them, said they should be at home helping him out. Of course, you see, they were his children there wasn't much anyone could do.'

He took another sip of tea, then, waving the half-full cup dangerously in the air, continued, 'As it turned out, the youngest, Liza, she didn't fare too badly. Bright little thing apparently, cottoned on fast that her daddy really wasn't all that interested in girls and did everything she could to make up for it. Right little tom boy by all accounts. Oh, there's no doubt, Liza became her father's favourite. The other one though, Emma, that was a different story.'

Tynan shook his head. 'I've never been able to make that out,' he said. 'How someone can love one child and be cruel to the other.'

Embury was gesturing with the teacup again, seemingly impatient with Tynan's interpretation of events. 'No, no,' he said: 'I don't think it was that at all. It wasn't that he didn't love them, just that he lacked the emotional capacities for showing it in any normal way.'

'I'm not sure I follow,' Tynan said. 'From what I understand he was violent when drunk and frequently drunk.'

'And as frequently remorseful,' Embury added. 'Oh, yes, a familiar enough pattern. Then at other times he'd be sober for weeks and months together. Worked hard, lavished everything he had on his children.' He shook his head sadly. 'Strange how a man can change in that way. It's no wonder the ancients believed in possession by demons.'

236

Tynan laughed shortly. 'I thought your lot still did.'

Embury returned the laugh. 'Well, let's just say most of us are pragmatic about it. It makes for a good bit of theological explanation when all else fails.'

'So,' Tynan asked, 'do you think he killed her?'

Embury shook his head slowly. 'I really wouldn't like to be the judge of the man. I knew him almost at second-hand, met him only a couple of times. You see, they'd moved out of the parish by the time I took over.'

'Where did they go to, can you remember off-hand?'

Embury thought about it for a moment, then said, 'I believe it was out Ancaster way somewhere. I don't remember exactly where.'

Tynan nodded. Ancaster. It was close to Ancaster that the itinerant woman they'd been looking for had nearly been run over by a car. He asked, 'So where did you get to meet him then?'

'Oh,' Embury said, 'he came back to the village often enough. Sometimes drunk, sometimes sober. Haunted the Greenway like one of its legendary fey folk. Last place his daughter was seen, you see. I suppose it played on his mind. Later, of course, when Liza went back to live with him, he seemed to settle down, or maybe she just stopped him coming. I don't know.'

'Went back?' Tynan questioned.

'Yes. When all the trouble blew up Liza was about seven years old. She went back to her grandmother's while it was being sorted out and stayed there until she turned eighteen or nineteen.'

'Then back to her father.'

Embury nodded. 'Presumably she felt some sense of duty to him, I don't know. She never married, though according to what I've heard she was a pretty girl. He wasn't capable of taking care of himself, that was for sure. His mind went, you know.' Embury paused, tapped his grey head meaningfully. 'Everyone said it was the drink, and I don't suppose that helped, but me, well, call me sentimental if you like, but I think it was grief. It's because of that I maintain that he loved his daughter. Drove him mad when he thought she was gone.'

He looked sharply at Tynan as though expecting some sort of confirmation. 'Grief, or maybe guilt,' Tynan said.

Embury shook his head fondly. 'That's the policeman in you talking,' he said. 'Suspicious to the last.'

'Maybe,' Tynan agreed, 'but it is a consideration.' He thought for a moment, then asked, 'What happened to the daughter, Liza, when her father died? I mean,' he added, 'I am presuming that he is dead?'

Embury nodded. 'Oh, dear, yes,' he said. 'Died about nine or ten years ago. Must have hit her hard, Liza. Lived for her father she did.'

'Did he still visit the Greenway?' Tynan wanted to know.

'Oh, yes.' Embury nodded enthusiastically. 'Every time he could get away from Liza. Watched him, I suppose, but no one could watch him all the time. He'd go missing, she'd come looking and there he'd be, wandering up and down, looking for Emma.'

Tynan tried not to show the growing excitement he was feeling. This was a link. It had to be. He said as casually as he could, 'Must have been a frightening sight, some old man, obviously off his head, roaming up and down the pathway like that?'

Embury looked keenly at him as though not certain where Tynan was headed but willing to guess. 'I suppose it might,' he responded cautiously, 'though most of the older folk knew he was harmless enough.' He paused, looked thoughtfully at Tynan. 'If you're thinking of linking him up with the Ashmore girl I feel you'd be doing the dead a great disservice. There was enough said about Cooper in his lifetime. It seems a little distasteful, don't you think, to try and make him a scapegoat now for something more?'

Tynan frowned. 'Come now, you know me better than that.' He paused, smiled encouragingly and prepared himself to ask Mike's other question, knowing that he was probably in for a long and meandering explanation. 'A place like the Greenway, all the stories there are attached to it. You think there's any truth in them?'

Embury perked up visibly, much to Tynan's inner distress. 'Oh,' he said, 'some of them undoubtedly have truth on their side. Now what particularly did you want to know?'

It was several hours later when Tynan finally took his leave and began the drive back to his own cottage.

He'd enjoyed the afternoon, for all that he felt he'd learnt nothing very useful after the first half-hour or so. Embury was, when once set in motion, an excellent raconteur with an infectious enthusiasm. Tynan, after his first misgivings had been fascinated by the legends and traditions, not just of the Greenway and Tan's hill, but which seemed to underpin the history of the entire region.

He let himself in to his home and reached immediately for the telephone. It took time to reach Mike, the desk sergeant had been uncertain as to whether or not he was even in the building. As it turned out he had just returned. Tynan heard the familiar voice, slightly puzzled, on the other hand.

'Hello there, Mike, it's John. Thought it best just to say it was a personal call.'

'Oh, right,' he said. 'Just took me by surprise, that's all. How did it go?'

'Well. Very well, but there's too much to tell over the phone. Later?'

'Yes. That's fine. But it will be around nine before I'm finished here.'

Tynan paused before asking. He could hear the tiredness but also the suppressed excitement in Mike's voice.

'You've found something else?' he asked.

Mike sighed. 'I had the search of the hidey hole extended. There's a second body, John, hidden deep under the hedge. It's only skeletal, of course . . .'

Tynan's voice sounded cramped, hoarse. 'Suzie?' It

was little more than a whisper. 'Suzie. After all this time.'

'We don't know for certain, John, but the chances are . . .'

'Oh, God.' A mix of relief and horror swept over Tynan. He'd not realized until now just how strong had been the irrational hope that Suzie might be alive somewhere. Not finding the body at the time . . . He felt sick, suddenly weak, as though from long illness. Found though, that he was clutching at the telephone as though it formed a link to sanity. To safety.

'John? Are you all right?' Mike's voice, grave and anxious floated to him from the receiver.

'Yes, yes, I'm all right.' He put the phone down and as though his legs were suddenly unable to give him support, slumped to the floor beside the telephone table. Then, John Tynan bent forward, cradled his face in his hands and wept for a child he'd never even known.

Chapter Twenty

Mike's day had not been an easy one and the telephone conversation with Tynan added to his sense of frustration. He wanted to go to the older man. His affection and liking for Tynan having grown out of all proportion to the short time the friendship had existed. Instead he had to put the phone down and hurry to answer the summons from Flint and his new temporary supervisor, CDI Peters. The best he could manage was to grab Bill in the corridor, tell him to phone Tynan, check that he was all right and assure him that they would be with him later. His meeting with Flint and the CDI, Peters, who was now heading the case took quite a time and it was, in fact, gone nine before Mike managed to get away and begin the half-hour drive out to Tynan's cottage.

He'd be able to confirm one thing when he got there. Suzie Ashmore's dental records were already at the lab from the match they'd attempted with the first skeleton. They'd run a match this time and there could no longer be any doubt.

The parents had been informed. Peters had arranged a press release to go out ready for the morning editions.

He'd not managed lunch with Maria Lucas. Too

much going on. But the brief conversation they had when she drove out to the village had been revealing. She'd then gone on to the caravan to assure the Thomases that Cassie was calm, that she was severely stressed and confused but not psychotic.

'I've arranged for her to stay on at Oaklands as a voluntary patient,' she told Mike. 'We're working with her, trying to fit together exactly what did happen. The big problem is, half the time she can't distinguish fact from the dream memories. But on the points I've given you, she's absolutely adamant.'

Mike reviewed those factors in his mind once more as he drove. He'd just spent over an hour chasing them round in circles with Peters and Flint and was no longer sure he had things exactly straight himself.

Her story fitted the facts though.

Suzie, she said, had found something. That much she had always known. Suzie had told her that she had a secret and that it meant they couldn't play in the hidey hole, a favourite place in previous summers.

It had been clear that whatever Suzie's secret was, it scared her. But Cassie – ten-year-old curiosity getting the better of her – added to Suzie's self-importance in knowing something really special. So Suzie had promised to show her.

They had gone one day to the hidey hole, been about to pull the brambles aside when suddenly her cousin had grabbed Cassie's arm and whispered furiously at her to run. Scared by her cousin's tone, Cassie had done as she was told. 'What are we running from?'

she'd asked finally, when they'd slumped down on the grass the village side of the Greenway.

'That man in the field. Didn't you see him?'

Cassie hadn't. 'He chases kids,' Suzie had told her. 'He chased me once.'

They hadn't attempted to go to the hidey hole again and taken short cuts through the Greenway only very reluctantly and always at a run.

Mike had reviewed the Ashmore case often enough for something in this to stick in his mind. Searching again, he'd found it. Two tiny references discounted at the time as irrelevant.

The first was a seemingly minor incident about a month before, when Mrs Ashmore remembered Suzie coming home in a panic because someone had chased her. She'd reported it to the police when Suzie had gone, thinking it might be important, but the track had been thrown very understandably when a local farmer came forward saying he thought it might have been him that frightened Suzie. She'd been with a group of kids, he said, pinching peas from one of his fields.

He stated that he'd shouted at the kids and chased them off. He'd been across the other side of the field at the time, no real threat, but Suzie might not have recognized him and been scared.

The other kids involved came forward somewhat reluctantly to confirm the story and the whole thing was passed off as irrelevant.

The second clue had come from Cassie herself. When the searchers had found her, she'd said something about a man and a woman, shouting, chasing them.

She'd later been questioned about them but couldn't even remember making such a statement. She'd seemed so confused when she'd been found that everyone assumed she'd banged her head, suffered concussion and imagined the people. So it had also been ignored.

Now, however, she'd been talking about them again, still not able to completely catch the memory and hold it fast, but, Mike thought, it still had significance.

He wondered again about Tynan, about his interview with the historical Mr Embury and what it might have turned up.

Were the Coopers linked to this? If so, how?

He gave up on the speculation as Tynan's cottage came into view. Bill had beaten him to it. Mike was glad of that, knowing that Bill Enfield's calm manner would have done much to help Tynan's shock.

There was one more thing, well one among many, that still puzzled him. The little pile of clothes in the back of the locked police car. That, and more importantly, the woman. Was the woman whose body had been so savagely attacked Liza Cooper?

Tynan opened the door and stepped back silently to allow him to enter.

'John. You're all right?'

The older man nodded curtly as though resenting this indicator of weakness. Then he sighed, relaxed.

'Yes,' he said. 'Can't think what came over me but suddenly it was such a shock.' He looked properly at Mike for the first time. 'How long before we know for certain?'

'We already do,' he said. 'Suzie's medical and dental

records had already been brought in for comparison. The dental records match. There was also a healed break to the right arm, she broke it about six months before she died. There's no doubt now.'

Tynan swallowed convulsively as though he wanted to be sick. 'How?' he asked. 'Do we know how?'

Mike hesitated. 'We've only got the preliminary reports,' he said gently. 'But it seems the same as the other one.'

Tynan looked questioning and Mike remembered belatedly that he didn't know how the other child had died. Mike himself had only found out a few hours before.

'Strangulation,' he said. 'Probably manual. It's a little early for specifics, but in both cases the hyoid bones are broken.'

Tynan had gone white, for a moment Mike thought he was going to faint. But he recovered and spoke very quietly. 'Can you imagine how scared she was, Mike, not being able to breathe, choking, seeing her killer's face . . .?'

'John!' All afternoon Mike had been trying not to think along those lines. He turned sharply, taking the older man by the shoulders and shaking him slightly. 'That's enough,' he said gently. 'You think I don't know what you're feeling, but it does no good.'

He released Tynan, could see Bill, just emerged from the sitting room, his face grave. He moved towards the kitchen and Mike could hear him filling the kettle as he shepherded John Tynan into the sitting room, got him settled in one of the big armchairs.

'Now,' he said, his tone suddenly businesslike. 'You said you'd got something to tell me. How did it go with Embury?'

He saw Tynan relax a little, try and get his thoughts in order, preparing to recount what Embury had told him about the Coopers. Then, abruptly, his shoulders sagged once more and he looked across at Mike, his face stricken by some sudden thought. 'Oh, God, Mike. Here's me making all this fuss. Can you just imagine how the parents are feeling? After all this time, all the grieving they must have done already and now it's starting all over again.'

Mike reached over, touched Tynan's arm, his hand light, almost reluctant. 'At least it can be over now, John. At least they know for certain.'

For a long moment Tynan stared at him, then said harshly, 'Does knowing that it's over really make you grieve less?'

Mike drew back as though Tynan's words had been some physical assault. His mind filled suddenly with images of Stevie. With despair at the waste of it all.

'No,' he said softly. 'I don't think it does.'

Chapter Twenty-One

Mike had been up since dawn but his first efforts to get the information he wanted were frustrated by the fact that bureaucratic institutions are not such early starters.

He'd stayed the night at Tynan's, too tired, apart from anything else, to want to make the run back along unlit, twisting, single track roads. He'd gone to sleep thinking, not about the enquiry, but, perversely, that he should look up details of furniture auctions, get himself a dining table.

Somehow, a dining table seemed more important, should he invite Maria Lucas to dinner, than the fact that his culinary abilities lifted themselves little above skill with a tin opener and a microwave oven.

He'd slept deeply, unplagued by nightmares, and woken thinking about the Coopers. Something told him that the woman, he'd begun thinking of her now as Liza, was not the homeless itinerant they had first thought. Her pattern of movements, the way she seemed not to drift far from some centre around Ancaster, pointed at least to a base. Could she have hidden Sara Jane there? Keeping her for the full five days in the hidey hole just didn't seem possible. There would be traces. Human faeces maybe, some smell of urine, and some kind of covering for the child. It may be late summer, but nights this close to the coast were often chilly.

No, she had to have been kept somewhere else and brought back to the Greenway.

Mike wasn't sure he wanted to speculate as to the reasons. Would she have been a third pathetic burial under the hawthorn? Did Cassie disturb the would-be murderer? Did Cassie kill the woman?

They'd come this far and still so many questions.

If Cassie didn't commit the murder, then who did?

He thought further, lying in the soft guest bed at Tynan's, watching light penetrate slowly through a crack in the thick curtains.

If Liza had a base then why hadn't it been found during the search? True, Ancaster, four miles away from the abduction, was outside the main search area, but even so, Mike had ordered a much broader sweep of all outbuildings and derelict properties.

Had someone simply not done their job? Or, more likely, had someone assumed that the relevant building fell in someone else's briefed area.

Either could be true, but Mike thought there might be a third possibility. Suppose it was simpler than that. Liza had moved back with her father, moved to some place out towards Ancaster. Well, wasn't it simplest to assume she was still there, given to wander perhaps and, after a lifetime of tending to a sick and deeply disturbed old man, perhaps not quite in the same universe that Mike inhabited, but, nevertheless, still there.

It made sense. The Coopers had evidently dropped out of sight and out of mind. Mike would be less surprised at this happening in a town, where anonymity and social invisibility could be had with ease. Here, where communities were theoretically much more tightly bound, it seemed odd that a middle-aged woman could be so unrecognizable even to her neighbours, that her picture in the paper brought reports only of a wandering gypsy selling clothes-pegs.

Where did she buy food? What doctor was she registered with? The questions went on. Finally, Mike argued himself back to the centre. People see and hear what they want and expect to see and hear. The police reports had asked for news of a wanderer. A tramp of no fixed address, not Liza Cooper, resident of . . . wherever. Practicably, he'd got only reports of an ageing itinerant. The explanation could be as simple as that.

He thought too of the description Tynan had given him of Embury's place. Isolated, several miles from the village whose postal address it would be using. Suppose wherever it was the Coopers lived was similarly isolated? They could be easily forgotten, particularly as, it seemed, they'd made every effort on their own part to withdraw from society.

Mike sat up, swung his legs over the side of the bed and slipped into the robe Tynan had lent him.

How to find out.

As quietly as he could, he padded downstairs and made for the telephone and drew a frustrating blank.

The recent electoral register didn't list any Coopers out at Ancaster.

'Some people do fall through the net,' the duty sergeant told him. 'It does happen, sir.'

Mike thanked him and put the phone down. No alternative now but to wait for the records' office to open. He decided to dress, leave a note for Tynan and then go and camp outside until someone turned up. Was about to do the first of these when Tynan himself appeared on the stairs.

'I'm sorry,' Mike apologized. 'I tried not to wake you.'

'You didn't.' He smiled, though with not quite his usual cheerfulness. 'I've been lying awake for over an hour. Afraid when I heard you using the phone, curiosity got the better of me.'

Mike laughed. 'I've been trying to find the Coopers' old address. But it looks as though I'm going to have to wait for other people to get up.'

Tynan smiled, and nodded. 'Well,' he said, 'at least it leaves time for breakfast.' He paused, thoughtful. 'I would guess it's likely to be another long day.'

The dream had elements of the real and the surreal blended so perfectly that Cassie didn't even try to distinguish them.

She walked across dew-laden grass, bare feet leaving

dry, perfectly patterned footprints in the bejewelled surface. She was in a garden, but a garden so overgrown that wilderness had reclaimed the neat borders, the herbs, the vegetable patch, and nettles grew between the tines of a fork laid down and long ago left to rust.

Cassie turned, walked now on a brick pathway. Moss and flaking brick clung to her feet, seemed to work their way between her bare toes, but she paid no attention. Pushing her way through a tangle of fruit trees and raspberry canes, she made her way not to the house but to one of the outbuildings off to its side. From within the shed came soft sounds, like some small animal. The door stood half open allowing a shaft of light to fall on the unconscious body of a child lying on a pile of straw.

Cassie looked back towards the house. From an upper window a man looked out. Not at the shed but at some vague point far off in the distance. As Cassie moved across the yard, he looked down, but there was nothing in his eyes or in his movement to say that he had seen her. Her or anything.

She paid him no attention, walked instead to the woodpile and lifted a piece which looked light enough to handle easily, heavy enough for her purpose. Then she crossed to the half-opened wooden door and stepped inside.

The woman from her dream knelt there, beside the child, one hand moving softly on the soft blonde hair; the other holding a light brown stocking. Her voice soft, tender, she sang softly to the motionless child, bending with an almost maternal care to kiss the sleeping face, then, with equal care, began to slip the stocking under the child's head, arranging it carefully, tenderly, about the child's throat.

Cassie waited no longer. There was no anger as she hit out, struck the woman as hard as her strength would allow on the right temple.

The woman, stunned, but still conscious, staggered to her feet, turning as she did so to face Cassie full on. As Cassie hit out again the woman raised an arm to protect her head. In Cassie's dream, the arm shattered under the blow, the force of it sending the woman reeling to the floor. This time, as she tried to rise once more, Cassie lashed out at the woman's head, striking the neck with all the force she could place behind it. The woman fell forward, landing face down on the concrete floor, trailing a glistening arc of blood that gleamed dull red in the early light.

As she hit out again the ground seemed to shift, to shimmer beneath her feet and Cassie found herself standing, warm sunlight of early morning warm upon her back, at the foot of Tan's hill, while up above her on the hill itself, she could hear two children laughing, saw Suzanne Ashmore and another child, smaller, darker, run hand in hand towards the Greenway.

Cassie woke. There was none of the panic, not a hint of the fear, the terror that had accompanied her previous dreams. Instead, she felt peaceful, supremely calm.

As Mike Croft sat in Tynan's kitchen, trying to

concentrate on breakfast and waiting impatiently for the day to begin, Cassie Maltham turned over in bed and went back to sleep feeling better – far better – than she had in years.

Nine o'clock saw Mike in the records' office waving his I.D. at a bemused clerk. Nine-oh-five had him dealing with someone who actually knew what they were doing and a search being made for the relevant documents.

By ten he had bypassed Flint and was explaining his position to Peters and by early afternoon he was heading out of Norwich in the area car, a squad car following, travelling towards Ancaster.

There Mike discovered that his problems were just beginning.

His assessment had been correct. The house the Coopers had moved to was isolated. The Coopers themselves had reinforced this isolation and it took almost an hour of wrong turns and misinformation before Mike finally drove up a dirt track and up to a rusting iron gate.

Mike stood beside the gate, suddenly hesitant, watching for any signs of movement, but the front windows of the house looked utterly blank, looked also as though shutters had been closed on the inside, forbidding any glimpse of its inhabitants to the outside world.

Mike marvelled at just how cut off from the world the

two had become. This house was less than two miles from Ancaster and yet it might have been in another world. The woman at the post office, from where they'd finally got directions to this forsaken place, had been voluble when once set in motion.

'No one goes there you see. It's not that we don't care, you understand, but they don't encourage help. She comes in here sometimes, but not often and when she does . . .' She waved a hand in the air as though trying to dissipate smoke.

'Well, you know, the smell. I don't suppose she's bathed in years.'

'You say no one goes there,' Mike queried. 'What about post?'

'What post? Must be years since they got any. Lord alone knows how they live. They say there's money hidden all over the house, but,' she laughed as though at some common joke, 'I doubt any self-respecting thief'd want to break in there. I mean, you never know what you might catch.'

Mike had let her run on a bit, then taken his leave and they had made their way out here. They, she'd said . . .

Thoughtfully, he looked at the house again. No gas, no electricity, no mains water. Apparently there was a well in the garden, so the postmistress had informed him and given him a lecture on comparative water quality into the bargain.

There was something else his search at the records' office had told him. There had been issued no certificate of death for Albert J. Cooper either a decade ago, or since. Could Liza have buried him somewhere and not notified death?

He picked the gate up, lifting it on its single rusting hinge and swung it awkwardly aside, led the four constables with him through the overgrown front garden and down the side of the house into the brick-floored yard at the back.

'You two,' he directed, 'try the house doors.'

He directed the others towards the attached outbuildings and stood in the centre of the yard looking around him at the devastation that had once been a home.

A flicker of movement caught his attention and he gazed up at the dark upper windows. Curtains half-hung, half-sagged from overstretched wires. One pair closed completely, the others slightly parted. He peered hard, willing whatever he'd half seen to move again. The two constables had circled the house and come back to the rear door.

'No open windows, sir, and the front door's probably bolted.'

He nodded impatiently. 'Then you'd better try the back, break the blasted thing down if you have to.'

He saw them exchange a glance and turned away, he couldn't blame them for not wanting to go in. Even from outside the place stank, though from the look of it, they'd have little problem with the door, even from where he stood he could see that it was rotting on its hinges.

'Sir, I think you'd better look.'

The officer emerged from one of the brick-built sheds looking more than a little sick. Mike walked swiftly over and went inside. Until the officer had disturbed it the door had been firmly shut and the full impact of the smell hit him like some solid, suffocating force.

'Christ Almighty.'

'Yes, sir,' the young man said, eyes watering in sympathy.

Mike pushed the door open to its fullest extent and stepped back to survey the scene from outside, reaching into his pocket for the flashlight he'd remembered to bring this time. This was the place. Nothing was more certain.

Human excrement littered one corner, in another lay a heap of filthy, decaying blankets and old sacking. Even from here they stank of urine. But what clinched it for Mike, what put beyond doubt that this was the place Sara had been kept, was the narrow strip of pale blue ribbon tied around a little tail of fair hair. Someone had fastened it to a nail hammered into the shed wall. More than anything else in this hell-hole, that sickened him the most . . .

'Sir.' The young officer was pointing. Mike looked; above the narrow window hung two more scraps of faded ribbon, one red and one green. One, tied carefully around a strand of dirty blonde hair, straight, without a hint of curl and about six inches long. The other, the green, encircled a delicate flowering of dark brown curls. The ribbon was frayed and rotten but someone . . . Liza? . . . had taken care to keep the soft curls free of cobwebs, of the thick layer of dust and grime that overlaid everything else.

Sadly, he stepped back outside, and let his gaze travel thoughtfully around the weed-infested yard. The other officer emerged from his search of the other buildings, pulling cobwebs from his clothes and hair.

'What's in there?' Mike demanded. 'Apart from spiders.'

The constable grinned, grateful to find some relief from the grim reality of the situation.

'An old pram. Funny thing is, sir, it's clean. Well,' he amended, 'sort of clean, like it's been used recently.'

Mike nodded. Had it been used to take Sara back to the Greenway? He was about to take a look for himself when a call from the house made him turn.

'He's here, sir. In one of the bedrooms.'

Mike strode across the yard. 'Alive?'

'Yes, sir.'

He pushed by the officer and began to climb the stairs, hearing behind him the officer remark, 'Just how can people stand to live like this?'

He tried to be professional enough not to ask himself such daft questions, but even so . . . the smell, the amount of dirt . . . Mike found it hard to comprehend.

The other constable stood uncertainly outside the door to the bedroom. Mike entered and motioned him inside. The room was dark, half-shut curtains and windows coated both inside and out in decades of grime added to the gloom. An old man sat at the end of the bed. Despite his surrounding conditions and his age, there was nothing emaciated or decayed about him. There was still a sense of strength, of purpose, of sternness in the way he sat, square-shouldered and straight-backed.

'Mr Cooper?' Mike spoke gently, uncertain of what approach to take.

The man did not speak, but turned his eyes directly onto Mike. Mike felt a moment of almost superstitious panic, felt the young man at his side flinch, as though the look had been directed at him.

'I knew you would come.' The voice was husky as though long out of use, but there was no weakness in it. 'I told her there was no other way. She should have let me see to it like last time.' He shrugged slightly as though resigned to the fact that life always let him down.

Mike waited, fearful of breaking the thread.

'She said she'd see to it this time, said she'd take her to the hill, do it there, but I never believed her. Weak, she was. Just left the child there, under the hedge for just anyone to find. Thought she could come back and lie to me, but I won't hold with that. Not with lying. So I followed her.'

He looked down at the floor then as though he'd said all he wanted to say. Mike had stood, frozen, as the man spoke. Suddenly, he was terrified that he would say no more. That he would refuse to speak and the rest of the story would remain untold. With difficulty, he held back on the impulse to shout, to demand, instead he spoke softly, words dropping gently into the stillness, 'And so you killed her.'

The man lifted his head again, eyes widened as though surprised that Mike should want clarification.

'Of course I did. What else was there to do? I knew she'd lied to me so I took wood from the woodpile.' He paused sadly, then went on. 'I didn't have time for the child. There was a woman running down the hill and I could hear people shouting so I came home.'

'And the wood you hit her with,' Mike asked. 'What did you do with that?'

Cooper glared at him indignantly as though the question were beneath contempt. 'Not a countryman, are you?'

Mike was startled but he answered slowly, 'No, I'm not.'

'Ah. I thought not. Wouldn't need to ask such damn fool questions if you were.' He paused, then, speaking slowly and patiently he said, 'Firewood belongs on the woodpile. I put it back there ready for winter.' He shook his head despairingly at Mike. 'Young folk. No idea, have you? Think I'd go wasting good firewood?' He shook his head again and stared down at the floor in fixed concentration. He did not even move to protest as Mike took his arm and led him away to the waiting car.

Chapter Twenty-Two

It was two more weeks before the funerals of Suzanne Ashmore and Emma Cooper took place. Suzanne's, in a large urban cemetery in the city where her parents now lived. Emma's in the churchyard of the village where her short life had ended so tragically. Mike attended both, so did John Tynan.

Suzie Ashmore's passing was well attended. Mike stood well back out of the way of those who had more right to be there. It was a bright September afternoon with just the slightest touch of autumn licking the trees that lined the route to the crematorium.

The service had begun when he saw Cassie and Fergus slip quietly into the church and stand almost unnoticed at the back. Suzanne's mother turned once to look at them, then turned away, her back a solid wall of disapproval. Mike shook his head sadly. He supposed it was too late to heal this kind of breach, founded as it was purely on grief, and beyond reason. He looked across and smiled at Cassie. Dr Lucas said that her recovery was exceeding all expectations, that she was ready to begin her life again. Mike was glad for them, for himself too. His friendship with Maria Lucas was blossoming and although he sensed that it

261

would be a long time before either of them was ready to make a commitment, he felt that he too was beginning his life over.

He pulled his mind somewhat reluctantly back to the present, aware that the service was almost over and that he should at least try to find the right page in the hymn book.

Behind him there was a slight draught and a soft thud. He knew that Cassie and Fergus had chosen their moment to leave.

The life and death of Emma Cooper was celebrated quietly a few days later. A couple of photographers turned up to record the event which warranted a paragraph or two in the local papers but other than that the funeral party was made up of Mike, Tynan and the others whose lives had been so shadowed by the consequences of this child's death.

It was on Mike's mind that in a few days' time there would be another funeral. That of Albert Cooper, found hanged by a bed sheet in a remand cell.

And, thought Mike, irritably, he'd said not a word more about anything since their brief conversation that day at the Coopers' cottage.

He stood between the Thomases and the Malthams as Emma's body was consigned once more to the earth, thinking how different this had been from the funeral of Suzie Ashmore.

He looked across at the Cassidys. Quite a number

of the local people had sent flowers, some attended the church service, but only the Cassidys had come to the graveside. Mike watched them as they stood there, keeping close to each other, their daughter safely between them. He thought how differently it might all have turned out . . . then forced himself not to think about it and bent with the others to drop a handful of earth into the grave.

It was only as they left the churchyard that Mike noticed Cassie. She still held flowers in her hand.

'Did you forget?' he asked her. 'I'll walk you back up if you want.'

Cassie smiled at him and shook her head. 'We've already left flowers on the grave,' she said. 'I want to take these to Tan's hill. It's just my way of finishing things properly.'

'We'd like you to come too,' Fergus said. It was an invitation that evidently included Tynan as well.

They walked in silence for several minutes, an odd, solemn procession. Then Anna asked, 'Do we know why he took Sara?'

Mike shook his head. 'We can only make guesses,' he said. 'I talked to her after Cooper was arrested, she remembered seeing him there once, on Tan's hill, or rather, she remembered seeing an old man talking, she thought, to himself. It scared her and she ran away.'

'Maybe he thought she'd found the body, same as Suzie did?'

'Maybe, we'll never know now.'

Anna nodded slowly. Simon reached across and

took her hand. He'd been unusually silent until now. 'It might seem far-fetched but have any of you noticed how like Suzie she looks? Sara Jane, I mean. Seeing her there, on the hill, it must have been as if she'd come back to haunt him.'

No one commented, it didn't seem necessary and Mike, for one, had developed a superstitious caution against violating the mystical aspects of this whole business. There were still so many things he didn't understand, like the child's clothes in the back of the police car and that strange dream Cassie had related to him when he'd gone to see her the day after Cooper's arrest. The meticulous and absurdly accurate detail she had been able to recall.

'You didn't do it,' he had told her, suddenly anxious that she might take on this further burden of guilt.

To his relief and surprise she had laughed. 'I know I didn't,' she said. 'But it felt good, like revenge without the consequences I suppose.'

They'd reached the mouth of the Greenway now. Anna stopped and sat down on the grass.

'Aren't you going any further?' Tynan asked her.

She shook her head. 'Call me superstitious if you like, but wild horses wouldn't drag me up there again.' Unconsciously, she moved a hand to touch her abdomen, already aware of the new life growing there.

Tynan smiled. 'You know,' he said, 'I'm not sure I want to go either.'

Anna patted the ground beside her. 'Have a seat.'

Mike, Fergus and Cassie began to walk on alone,

then Cassie stopped abruptly. 'I can't,' she said softly. Fergus turned to kiss her gently then took the flowers from her hand.

'Then let me.'

Cassie nodded, relieved, and they watched her as she walked the short distance back to the others.

Fergus and Mike stood for quite some time on the hill top. They'd placed the flowers where the hidey hole had once been. Already the hawthorn and brambles were growing back, healing the man-made wound that gaped in the hedge-side. Then they'd gone back and stood on the hill looking down at the Greenway, stretching out, straight but for the kink around the hill.

The afternoon was warm, a slight breeze keeping it from being hot. Far off out to sea there was a darkening, as though rain clouds gathered and already the strip of sea that they could glimpse from the hill top looked muddied, anticipating the dark of storm clouds.

'I think we should go now,' Fergus said, his voice sharpened slightly as though something troubled him.

As they hurried back along the pathway, it seemed to Mike that there was a slight shimmering in the air, like a displaced heat haze moving before his eyes and that the ground seemed to shift beneath his feet. The hedges – high and solid though he knew them to be – blurred suddenly as though seen through misted glass.

He felt panic rising, choking him, looked across at Fergus and saw the same emotions written on the other man's face.

Instinctively, they began to run, fleeing in

unashamed panic from a place that no longer welcomed them.

But it seemed that the sound of laughter pursued them down the high-hedged pathway, and, forcing himself to look back for an instant, Mike saw that two figures stood, small and childlike, against the blue sky on the crest of Tan's hill.